RUTH RUN

A NOVEL

ELIZABETH KAUFMAN

PENGUIN PRESS   NEW YORK   2025

PENGUIN PRESS
An imprint of Penguin Random House LLC
penguinrandomhouse.com

Designed by Meighan Cavanaugh

LIBRARY OF CONGRESS CATALOGING-IN-PUBLICATION DATA
Names: Kaufman, Elizabeth, 1967– author.
Title: Ruth run : a novel / Elizabeth Kaufman.
Description: New York : Penguin Press, 2025. | Summary: "An ingeniously twisty, witty,
and fast-paced cybercrime chase novel in which the eponymous thief, who has stolen several
lifetimes worth of money, flees Northern California and makes her way across Oregon, Idaho,
and Utah with a slew of men in pursuit, the relationships between herself and her male
pursuers shaped by the protagonists' respective interpretations of the traces each leave in the
cyberworld" —Provided by publisher.
Identifiers: LCCN 2024014884 (print) | LCCN 2024014885 (ebook) |
ISBN 9780593832646 (hardcover) | ISBN 9780593832653 (ebook)
Subjects: LCGFT: Thrillers (Fiction) | Novels.
Classification: LCC PS3611.A8264 R88 2025 (print) | LCC PS3611.A8264 (ebook) |
DDC 813/.6—dc23/eng/20240722
LC record available at https://lccn.loc.gov/2024014884
LC ebook record available at https://lccn.loc.gov/2024014885

Printed in the United States of America
1st Printing

for Analia, my favorite daughter

RUTH RUN

1

RUTH

THE COOKIE VANISHES

I was dreaming about a ginger cookie—soft-centered, crunchy with sanding sugar—when the alarms went off. It was three a.m., and somewhere someone had hit one of my electronic trip-wires, triggering phone alerts that shocked me awake. I flung my arm to mute them, then lost a moment wondering what thief falls asleep mid-thievery. In my defense, a yearslong cybercrime can get dull.

I checked my laptop. Someone had poked the software that transferred money from my East Coast accounts through the hacked firewalls. They'd halted a funds transfer. Had they found any of the offshore accounts? Either way, it was time to delete everything and go. Past time. My years of peaceful bank robbery were done. As I started removing scripts and scrubbing log files, I asked myself for the hundredth time: cover-up first or get-away? That answer should be in some crime FAQ. But a compelling advantage of digital theft is that your hunters rarely start where you live. Someone had discovered my work and was probably searching for me, but my apartment was dim and quiet. I ordered myself not to freak my shit. I still had time to clean up and get out. No one could see me here.

2

MIKE

WATCH HER RUN

Ruth adjusted her shoulder bag and turned a slow 360. She wore her brown jacket, jeans, running shoes, a plain white blouse. In the bag were two prepaid phones still in plastic, a charger, toothbrush, hairbrush, wallet and passport, a pen and a small yellow pad, two changes of socks and underwear, large sunglasses, a pink BIC lighter, one very good blond wig, a Red Sox cap, and $25,000 in twenty-dollar bills, still stacked tight in violet bank bands.

Early sunshine streamed into the room, illuminating the airborne dust. She stood and studied every surface. I knew she was wondering what she had forgotten, what was left to help a man hunting her. She'd swapped her hard drive for a backup full of card games and crochet animal patterns. The original she'd zeroed, baked in the oven, and shoved into her bag. She examined the books, stacked in no order on the crappy plywood shelves. Account numbers scrawled in the margins? No. Random, self-betraying scribbles? Impossible. But this situation was outside her experience. She had no idea how capable or relentless my team might be. Or who we were.

There wouldn't be much to find in that apartment: Goodwill plates and cutlery, plastic cups, a French press that made coffee at once weak and full of grit. Getting rich had been a lean process. The refrigerator remained empty. She ate packaged crap when she bothered to eat—an unholy assortment of turkey jerky and the occasional Trader Joe's frozen ethnic dinner. There was a cheap window bird feeder, and her father's old violin in its bright painted case on a side table. I'd been sure she would take it. How far did she expect to get, really, with me in pursuit? A flowered violin wouldn't sink her. With a little planning, she might even have stored it somewhere. But there it sat, and she walked away from it.

She couldn't be certain I'd found her hack or the complex web of scripts and small databases that overlay it. Her system looked innocuous if a person happened to stumble onto it; pieces were spread across the internet. But we must have triggered an alert. At 0300 hours, we'd probed the relays to her offshore account, and the first overnight transfer from the US banks had failed. The next began on schedule, but we'd spooked her. She had already started to dismantle everything, shutting it down. She must have planned to burn it all behind her someday. Still, she'd needed almost five hours to disable and delete the scripts and databases that had collected and directed her stolen fortune over the last forty-five months. The compromised microchips had to stay, of course, but they were useless without her knowledge. Somewhere she must have left me a clue to their access. It would be my challenge to find it.

Ruth closed her eyes. She always got away. That's how it worked. I'd made sure of it. This time, she expected to be staggeringly rich. The light caught her hair, her cheekbone, the curve of her ear. It was a face to be studied in black and white or while she slept. Awake in the world, she had the trick of blurring against her background like a rare nocturnal moth or the bird that hunts it. I memorized her face on the screen. It might be my last chance to look at Ruth before she could return my scrutiny.

She turned again, clockwise this time, unwinding herself from that room, that home, then walked out through the tiny kitchen, carefully locking the door behind her.

3

MIKE

HER FIRST
WRONG TURN

On the street, Ruth strode to her car. It was the dry season in Northern California. The sky was a relentless blue, and fuchsia bougainvillea sprawled across the trellised porches. She didn't stop to admire it. She didn't look for me. She climbed into her grubby Civic, started it, and pulled into the street. Then, at the stop sign, she hesitated. Parked around the corner, engine running, we waited for her to choose an escape route. I expected she would turn toward El Camino, work her way to Marsh Road, and go north on 101. She had an old cash-bought car parked along the way to trade into. I expected her to bolt out of the Bay Area, as much as anyone can bolt through that morning traffic. But there was still her assistant-in-crime, stupid hapless Thom. He had written most of the software for the theft. His name, with hers, was on the Caymans account. He'd be in his cubicle, staring at the mini crossword, waiting obliviously for the posse (that was us) to seize him.

It had been Ruth's first large heist; she had mishandled her subordinate. Thom had not received the alerts, did not have an escape plan. She should not have involved him in the first place. She should not risk herself to get him out. Too much to hope, in that moment, that she'd turn toward me. I knew she wasn't ready. I approved her loyalty but faulted her judgment trying to save Thom. That choice was her first hint of instability.

A honk behind her—Ruth startled and turned right. She was going to the office.

4

RUTH

NO BREAD IN MOAB

I love one thing more than money. Food. It's a fact about me. You know when you're lying there after sex and your partner asks: What are you thinking about? They want to hear "you" or "us" or "love," but my answer is always food. Not food in general. It's something specific: maybe a McIntosh apple warm off an autumn tree or a Neuhaus dark chocolate praline with a double shot of perfect espresso or a hot, fresh croissant. Of course, I don't share these thoughts. I'm aware my answer doesn't fit the storyline.

Years ago, I put aside my first love to go after my second. Because food can't buy money, but money can buy food and most other things as well, like security of sorts and free time and maybe a good dog with a yard to play in. Even things without price tags come easier when you're rich: health, friends, safety in the dark. Some people plan to sleep when they're dead; I've promised myself to eat when I'm rich. By that, I mean I'll eat what I want. In the meantime, food can't be important.

It's stupid to talk about life balance; distraction won't advance any serious goal. I think that balance shit comes from successful people trying to knock out competitors, tossing misdirection behind them like mental tack strips. Every person has a hard limit for focus, for effort, for love. No one is smarter eating Stumptown Cold Brew Coffee Ice Cream at the keyboard or spreading a ripe Brie de Meaux on a thin slice of toasted baguette (with a strip of prosciutto, a dab of fig preserve, and black pepper) while she checks undocumented gates in a microchip.

So I quit food, and I also gave up sex. It wasn't productive. When I'd first moved to California, I'd hooked up with the best microchip engineers I could find. They loved to lecture a girl about their work; their foreplay amounted to a short course in electrical engineering. Soon enough, I'd noticed their libraries were all the same and decided it was more efficient just to read the books. Hanging on some rich arm was never my goal. I always knew to get my own money, I'd have to put off everything else.

I had my failures, though. When I drove away from the Menlo apartment to collect Thom, I stopped at the corner, and all at once the car smelled like cheese bread. There's a Draeger's grocery there where they make loaves of asiago sourdough. Some days, I'd wandered through its bakery section, smelling the cheesy air, imagining eating a whole loaf. I never touched food like that, though. The time for good things would be after I was rich and safe. Still, the car suddenly smelled like asiago bread, and for a moment, I lost concentration. I forgot that someone might be coming for me, that I needed to find Thom and get out. Then some jerk honked, and I remembered where in life I was. So I turned toward the office, the place my hunters (if there were hunters) were sure to come. I drove my own car, wore my own hair, and carried almost three pounds of stolen cash. Brilliant.

5

RUTH

OPERATION NITWIT RESCUE

I was the senior product line manager for bank security at the world's largest network equipment company. You might know them. Maybe you've cursed their stock price or power-cycled one of their routers or office phones, or all of the above. After I designed my hacked microchip, I needed to get it onto a product that would give me access to lots of vulnerable banking systems. I got a job at that big company and had them integrate my chip with a turnkey system to bring legacy mainframes online, to defend them, and to steal from them.

My office was on the fourth floor in one of a series of mostly identical buildings on the San Jose campus. Thom's cubicle was in the same building, one floor down. I pulled into the parking lot and backed into a space with a view through the glass walls of the rear entryway. I sat behind the wheel and watched the building. Was it too busy? Too quiet? I'd planned my escape as a faraway exercise, not a sneaking-through-my-normal-life thing. I was going to have to improvise.

I collected my bag and stepped out of the car. A black SUV swerved into the lot and up to the back door. Two squared-off men in tan Dockers climbed out, went through the door, and turned toward the elevators. Each of them in turn pressed the call button. They really wanted an elevator. Silicon Valley had a lot of relatively harmless preppy men prone to double-pushing call buttons. Even so, I decided to take the stairs.

My bag was awkward, and the jacket too warm. Apparently I should have been jogging daily with pounds of money in a fanny pack. Another missed opportunity. As I got to the third floor, the fire door swung inward and those two men came through: half-inch government lanyards, name badges turned backward (the universal symbol for an out-of-bounds institutional goon), and sidearms. I ducked my head, stepped back, let my face settle into boringness. Their eyes skimmed past and down the stairwell. If they were looking for me, they were failing, but surely it was too soon. I stared vacantly at the carpet. "Hurry," said the man in back. They headed upstairs, and I stepped sideways through the closing door.

Thom wasn't in his cubicle. His red windbreaker was draped on the chair; his ID lay next to the keyboard. Toby in the next cubicle tipped his chair back. "He's not there."

He clicked his mechanical pencil in a worried way; the lead

was seriously overextended. "I see that," I said. "Where is he?" I didn't know what Thom had told him. I wasn't taking the time to find out.

Toby glanced around. He lowered his voice. "Some dude from security and a lady from HR came for him. I think they're in the conference room." He clicked his pencil again, pointed it toward the south end of the building, and we watched the lead fall onto the carpet. "They said it was urgent." What were the odds that slow Thom was mixed up in a second major white-collar crime?

"I bet I need him more than they do," I said. "If he gets back before I find him, please tell him to call me." And I picked up the ID and the jacket like that was a normal thing to do. "See ya." I half waved and turned away. Then turned back as Thom's screensaver came on. It was a photo of the pair of us, clearly and obviously on Seven Mile Beach, Grand Cayman, shading our eyes against the sun and laughing like, well, exactly like two people who had just robbed a bank—several banks, in fact.

The nitwit bastard! I'd been so clear about the need for secrecy. And I'd avoided cameras for years. When cell phones got them, it seemed that everyone's face would be everywhere, but people only want pictures of themselves. I became the photographer, never the subject. I couldn't know when or why I'd need to disappear; it just seemed inevitable. Now my only casual photo in the last six years was displayed brilliantly dead center of my flight path. What else might be on that computer? I had no good choices. I couldn't throw it out a window—they didn't open. I also couldn't smash it and flush the pieces down the toilet or light it on fire, not with Toby sitting right there. Rescuing Thom had been a weak impulse. I should have vaporized him months ago. I headed for the conference room.

From the hallway, I could see Thom through the glass, slumped and sorry-looking; a blond woman in glasses with statement frames, HR for sure; and an older guy dressed like a mall cop, both with company badges. No one had coffee; the woman had a pad and a big binder. Everyone looked tense. The door was half-open, and I guessed they were waiting for more people, maybe the Dockers brigade.

I'd always been a planner. This theft had taken years, first to design the hardware, then to get it into production, to ensure my target banks acquired it, to write the software (OK, to convince Thom to write the software), collect the money, store it in safe havens offshore, and always to watch my own back. I'm not complaining about the effort, just pointing out that I'd trained for my vocation like my colleagues trained for marathons, except I hadn't gone around bragging about it. Big success takes a big plan, but big plans have problems. It's hard to improvise—even in the gaps, the way out is usually predetermined. For example, it wasn't enough to extract Thom from the conference room; we needed to take the back stairwell and go through the Operations Center, if I was going to get us discreetly to my second car parked on that side of the lot. Also, I'd come to see that every secret casts a shadow. As things moved and changed around it, my plan stood still; eventually that stillness would draw attention. I'd read that predators react to motion, but I thought the people hunting me might be searching exactly for things in the wrong place, things that did not move. Then again, the dudes in the stairwell hadn't seemed too advanced.

I walked on to the conference room. I stuck my head in the door. "Sorry for this, but I need Thom now. We have a big outage."

Everyone turned to me. Thom sat up. "Oh," he said. "OK. I'd better come." He seemed surprised to see me. In fact, he seemed not entirely relieved. But he pushed back his chair.

The HR person had a very sweet voice. "We need Thom here. And you too, Ruth. Our guests just left to find you." Lash extensions, red power suit, manicured nails—I had less in common with her than with her cat, if she had one. Sometimes I thought, if a person like that was a woman, I must be something else. She patted the chair next to her. "Come sit." As if that worked on anyone but Thom.

I sighed. "Are your guests from Bank of America? Because the BofA network is down *right now*. They're bleeding millions." The HR woman said nothing. I shifted my bag. "We're on the same side," I told her. "I'll bring him straight back as soon as we fix this outage." I caught Thom's eye. "Come on," I said, and walked off toward the back exit, fast but not galloping, not looking over my shoulder, no obvious panic. Thom came along behind me. We went through the door and ran together down the stairs.

"Fuck," I said. "Fuck, fuck, fuck. Who were those men, Thom? What did they know? What did they ask you?"

"I thought you'd left," said Thom. "I didn't hear anything. I figured you'd taken off."

We reached the first-floor fire door. I snapped at him, angry, because leaving him should have been my first instinct. "You thought I ditched you? Seriously?" I waved his ID past the security reader. "I'm not that kind of asshole, Thom." The reader beeped, flashed red. I waved his badge again; the light again turned red. "Oh shit."

Thom reached over my shoulder. "Let me try." He held his badge against the reader. Third time red. "Try yours," he said. "They must have blocked mine." He reached across again and held my badge to the reader. It chirped green. We pushed through the door into the back of the Operations Center. *Home free*, I thought. At least I didn't say it aloud.

6

RUTH

WE ALL MAKE MISTAKES

Before I continue, let's agree there are shades of wrong. We're all somewhere in the mix. One person might rescue puppies and run red lights. Someone else might give half his paycheck to Greenpeace and also hit his kids. Do you see my point? Some wrongs are deliberate, while others are honest mistakes. That guy who put his greasy pizza box in the paper recycling—do you think he meant to ruin a whole truckload? No. He's a good person who made a mistake. And that's me too. I'm a good person; I just can't resist money when I see piles of it unguarded. And the other things I did? Those were like the pizza box guy—stupid mistakes.

I've seen people who steal for fun or because they can't stop themselves. I'm not in it for the stealing. I do it to get things the world wants to keep from me. As a kid, I took food when I was hungry. I didn't take it from people; I stole it from a store that was full of things to eat. They threw food in the dumpster every day, but why should I pick through trash? I stole Grey Goose if Mom sent me for Popov's; no reason to buy bad vodka when the good stuff was right there. Our world is full of excess—too much stuff, too many rules about it. So I work around those rules to get what I need. I'm skilled, and I'm careful. No one misses what I take. Maybe now you're judging me, but it's not like I mugged old people. I skimmed chump change from banks. Are you really going to side with a bank? I know if you could do what I can do, you would no shit have done what I did. I know it.

7

RUTH

IF PIPES COULD READ AND WRITE

I'm twenty-six now, and I learned the most important thing for my plan six years ago. I feel like a *Scooby-Doo* villain gloating about My Plan. But that's what it was. I'll skip the capital letters and twirling mustache. (Which I do not have, by the way. I'm a zero to look at. Forgettable. That bothered me when I was younger, but it's an advantage now. I work at my plainness.)

I was twenty and managing a big university data network in New England. They took a cheap chance hiring me after graduation—my minimal qualifications justified their minimal salary. I've always worked for a paycheck, though my priority was skills acquisition for my plan, once I had one. Anyhow, my first job was to manage that network and to make sure things like email ran properly.

The school connected to the internet through a single router, manufactured by the company, my last employer, that makes most of those things. I was trying to learn, so our router was actually an experimental product. Specifically, the board inside the router that connected our network to the internet was on limited distribution for testing.

One day I got a call from an administrator with an email problem. I went to check his machine, and there was a single message stuck in the queue that would not send. I did all the things. First I sent a different test from his machine to the same target address, and that worked, so I knew something was wrong with that particular email. I tried sending the stuck one to a different outside address, and it failed. I tried both from a different machine with exactly the same results. Then I sent the failing one to my own internal address, and it worked. For some reason, that one email could not leave our network. I cut the message in half—one part sent and the other failed. I continued cutting the failing message in half until I was down to a couple of words in a specific order that could not transit our router to the internet. It was a rare bug but a real one: I'd found a data sensitivity on our fancy test board. The onboard chip didn't understand English, but it had to read the sequence of bits that represented those words on the network. For some reason, it could not transcribe that specific pattern from our internal network across to the internet.

When we try to explain networks, we like to talk about

pipes. Who doesn't love plumbing? But networks are exactly *not* pipes. Every place a wire (or an antenna or a dish, with the air-based ones) enters a box and something goes out the other side, the hardware and software read, analyze, and make decisions about every piece of data. The hardware and software transcribe it and send it on. There's no useful comparison to a turd or dirty dishwater: the bits on a network are constantly analyzed and reconstructed. On our internet router, when the new microchip on the prerelease board identified a certain sequence, it dropped the whole transaction. Email is an all-or-nothing proposition. If part of the message couldn't go through, the entire thing got stuck. But what seemed like a weird email problem was actually bad behavior on a tiny microchip.

When I realized what was happening, I didn't yell *Gold!!!* and run right out of the room, tossing my pick and shovel in glee. For one thing, I'm restrained. For another, I didn't see right away how I could use any of this to get rich. I did sense there was a superpower somewhere: the microchips could access everything. They could do more than transcribe data from an inbound network to an outbound network; they were capable of misbehavior. I needed to figure out how to put that capability to use.

8

RUTH

I THINK I KNOW THAT GUY

The Ops Center was a large, open-plan area that covered most of the ground floor. The east side had a wall of screens dedicated to monitoring the high-value banking clients, with a couple rows of tables with chairs and large-display computers for the Operations staff. The west section, where we entered, was a data center that held hundreds of racks of servers and network gear dedicated to internal network services, client backup, and paid cloud operations. It was cool and poorly lit; we had to talk over the ambient roar of the fans.

I led the way almost to the far exit, then stopped and leaned against the back wall. I also hadn't rehearsed thinking and running. Thom stood with me. "What's happened with BofA?" he asked. "Is it connected to, you know, our stuff? I figured something was wrong when I saw you'd taken down the scripts."

Oh, if judging Thom were a drinking game . . . "There is no BofA outage. That was an excuse to get you away from them." I noticed his jacket and handed it to him. "Someone hit one of my tripwires last night. Two of them, actually. They probed an intermediate database. I was up all night deleting everything."

"Who's 'they'?" he asked.

"I don't know. Tiger Team, maybe? Bank security? Those guys don't look like normal cops." I studied his face. "Does it matter? It's time to go."

Thom straightened up. He swallowed awkwardly, extending his whole head and neck forward like a tortoise, and shifted his feet. I knew this routine meant he was working his way into an objection. Before he could say anything, across the room, the Dockers men came in through the main doorway. All five of them. "They're multiplying!" Thom said. We stepped behind the nearest equipment rack. He ducked down and whispered, "You go. I'll turn myself in. I can stall these guys until you're out of here."

I'd thought of leaving him, of course, but I hadn't considered him wanting to be left. Something was up. I was not in the mood to solve a little Thom-puzzle. "Look," I said. "You can turn yourself in any damn time you want. But we have maybe three minutes to get out of here. So let's please run while we can. You can unmake the run choice, but not the give-up one." He stood silently. I added, "These guys have guns."

Thom didn't answer, but the impulse to self-sacrifice, if that's what it was, receded. I peered around the rack just as another man entered the monitoring area—a past-his-prime Dudley Do-Right in a shiny suit. The other men turned toward him, pointing at the screen and gesturing back toward the racks of equipment. The boss had arrived. I stared at him. It was the suit, I think: I realized suddenly he would also be wearing fancy shoes. "I recognize that guy. Thom, what the fuck." I watched a moment longer. "And that's the security system they're looking at. They know we came in that door. They know we're here."

The man in the suit said something, and there was a click as the latch deployed in the door behind us. Thom grabbed my arm. "That's a system override," he hissed. "They just locked us in."

To be captured was not my plan. I did not accept that outcome. I try never to imagine failure, not because it's impossible, but because I think I'll summon it by thinking about it. That superstition comes from my mother. "Don't dwell on trouble," she'd say, then do it anyhow. So even while I prided myself on meticulous risk assessment, the actual manifestation and conjunction of multiple serious threats right then in a familiar place, when I should have been elsewhere, that was not OK. There had to be a way out. I looked up and noticed the red light blinking from a fixture above us. There it was. I grabbed the BIC lighter from my bag and pulled a twenty from the stack. I flicked the lighter once, twice, and the twenty flared. Nothing. Then Thom crouched and wrapped his arms around my waist. He wobbled, stood, and hoisted me up—the men were fanning out to start a search pattern through the equipment racks—and I held the smoldering bill up to the alarm sensor.

Three, two, one: a blaring horn clanged suddenly from everywhere; there was a loud hiss as the fire alarms triggered the sprinklers and, beneath the chaos, an emphatic click as the fire emergency system also unlocked every door in the building. The men started shouting.

"Go!" I said, and Thom pulled open the door. As we fled the Ops Center, I glanced back over my shoulder. The familiar man was still standing in the front of the room, water pouring from the sprinkler overhead, spoiling his suit. He was looking right at me. He raised his arm, and waved in a way that seemed almost friendly, a salute even. He mouthed something I couldn't hear. I ducked my head and I ran.

9

RUTH

MY PRIMARY FUCKUP

I can admit my mistakes. I made an obvious primary error, not in my plan but in my execution of it. That first oversight was the catalyst of most of the mistakes that followed. I'm not talking about my pizza-box-type error, a (large, granted) unintended consequence. I mean that I missed the moment when I won. I was rich enough long before that alarm went off. I had $250 million in safe havens offshore, $50 million in the Caymans, and the rest split between Switzerland and Belize. There'd been a time to elegantly withdraw, and I'd blown past it. My eyes were maybe bigger than my pockets. A person who knew how to have money would have disappeared much sooner. She'd have waited, far away and safe at her cherrywood desk with mountain views, picking at an amuse-bouche of baby crab claws dipped in edible wasabi candle wax, while her private army of seasoned pros deployed to perform Thom-rescues as necessary. If necessary. I think people skilled at being rich are also better at disposing of accomplices.

WE RAN ACROSS THE ENTRYWAY, out the emergency door, and into the parking lot. I stopped at a vintage maroon Saab with a 26.2 decal in the back window. I pulled the key from the exhaust pipe and unlocked the doors. "Get in!" Thom got in.

I spun out of the parking lot as quickly as I dared. No point being inconspicuous now.

"Ruth." Thom did his swallowing thing. "Where are we going? Do you even have a plan?"

I turned right, sped to the corner, ran the red, and turned toward the highway.

"My plan," I said, "is to get away. That OK with you?" I merged onto 880 northbound and put my foot down, weaving through the late-morning traffic. Thom crossed his arms and sat back. I glanced at him. "What am I missing? Did I ruin your plan to go to prison? Shit." I swerved right and took the cutoff to 680. I started counting exits. "Thom, look, I know this morning has been horrible. I'm kicking myself that I left everything so late. We never should've had to run like that." He didn't answer.

I drove on, saving his sulky ass. I found the exit, left the highway, and turned onto the frontage road. I drove to the intersection and turned right. This spot had seemed sensible a year ago. Now every mile south felt like lost ground against our pursuers. I turned into a housing development, drove to number 43545, and parked the Saab, tossing the key onto the driver's seat.

"Come on," I said, "unless you want to wait for them here." I walked across the driveway, pulled the key from a gray Corolla, tossed my bag in back, and got into the driver's seat. Thom climbed in on the passenger side.

I reached around into my bag and pulled out the wig. It was premium human hair, medium golden blond with honey lowlights, part of the dream where I stepped elegantly into another world. It couldn't hurt to wear it. I settled it on my head and put on the sunglasses. Then I backed the car out and headed back toward the highway. "Check in the door pocket."

Thom reached his hand down and pulled out a bag. "Combos?"

"Pepperoni Pizza Combos. They aren't new. But they're probably as good as they ever were." I merged northbound, sedately now the cars were swapped. "Thom, forgive me. Please. Whatever it is. We can figure out next steps together when we're somewhere safe. I just don't think we should put those guys in charge of the rest of our lives. Whoever they are."

He opened the bag. Sighed. "Fair enough." He bit a Combo in half longitudinally and ate the filling. Then he sucked on the cracker pieces. He offered the bag, and I shook my head. I have my limits.

"Who was that guy? The one you said you knew. The dumpy one in the suit?"

"Well, he looked a lot like a salesman from my last company. I don't see how it could be him, though." I didn't mention the salute across the room as we'd run out. It sounded mad. "We called that guy Hydrant Mike."

"Hydrant Mike?"

"Yeah. One year, the holiday party was at the CEO's house in Carmel. He had this ancient tiny dog wandering around. She was pissing on people's shoes, if they didn't notice and shove her away."

Thom snorted.

"Yeah, she was kind of a canine cluelessness detector. Alert people didn't get marked."

"And Hydrant Mike got pissed on?" Thom had turned toward me, and tucked his left leg under his right.

"Sure did. And he wore expensive shoes. It was a scene." I drove north on 680, following signs to Walnut Creek and Sacramento. I wondered how that guy could have anything to do with my life now.

10

MIKE

CLEANUP CREW

I t took discipline not to chase her, to resist the summons im-
plicit in that shared look and her flight. I watched the livestream from Ruth's car as we drove to the apartment in Menlo
Park. Someone needed to take responsibility and pick up after
her. I knew enough about flight response to be sure she would
stop soon; she would stop, and turn back for me.

We were soaked. My hair dripped onto the screen. I worried
about my headphones. Only my driver, a consultant named Earl,
had managed to stay dry. Earl had a talent for evading consequences. He parked and said, respectfully enough, "We're here,
boss. Are you OK to come inside? We can pick them up after
we search the apartment. It's not like they're getting away." He
spoke loudly over the audio stream. Possibly he thought I was

deaf. "You won't miss much. We need you to recover the equipment."

I doubted Ruth's apartment would offer more information or interest than watching her drive and eavesdropping on her conversation with Thom. But I was the one who had installed the gear, so I was the man to recover it. Also I was drawn to Ruth's violin. I wanted to touch it for myself, investigate that flamboyant case. It was unreasonable to think she'd left it for me to find. There was no way she could know about my twelve years of Suzuki instruction. Nevertheless, the instrument was another bond between us. I put down the tablet, and took off the headphones. I covered them with Thom's windbreaker (recovered from the data center), swung my feet over Thom's knapsack, and climbed out of the SUV.

11

RUTH

BAD NEWS FROM ANNOYING THOM

We were passing San Ramon in traffic, and I heard the ting of an incoming text. I looked over and realized that Thom the Moron had turned on his iPhone to check messages.

"What the *fuck*, Thom! They can track that!" I swiped at it, but he shrunk back.

"Shit," he said. "I didn't think." But he hesitated and stared down at the screen. "You're going to want to hear this, though."

"Will you shut it off?" I asked him. I was remembering Marvin the Martian and his Illudium Q-36 Explosive Space Modulator. I was imagining blasting Thom to tiny bits with it. I was also thinking about a white-clam-and-garlic pizza I'd watched a friend eat once in New Haven. Maybe I'd go back to that restaurant and order the same pizza, after I space modulated Thom. I'd ask for lemon wedges and a very cold ginger ale. Then I'd go to Wooster Square and have a cannoli and a latte with a shake of cinnamon over the foam for dessert. I glanced at him. "What am I going to want to hear?"

Thom swallowed. "Toby says those guys searched my cubicle and took my knapsack."

I passed a red Prius with a POVERTY IS VIOLENCE bumper sticker. "Yeah? Is there something bad in there?"

"There's an AirTag." Thom waited a moment. Maybe he was giving me time to holster my mental Space Modulator. "Want me to check where it is?"

His phone had already pinged the local tower; our location was obvious to anyone tracking us. "Sure."

Thom checked his phone. "They're at your place, I think, in Menlo?" He looked again. "They must have left my bag in the car outside." He powered off his phone, and we drove for a while, considering that.

My apartment was not precisely secret, but I'd never shared the address. I had no lease and had paid cash for everything. The home address I gave at work was affiliated with a mailbox service in Mountain View; that same address was on my driver's license. In fact, my former home should have taken a moment to find. Thom had been there once or twice. He'd been my only guest.

"Hey, Thom?"

He turned.

"Is my Menlo address in your contacts?"

"I don't think I ever knew it."

"Not a dropped pin? Nothing?"

"No," he said. "Why? Don't you think HR gave it to them?"

"HR never had it."

"The cars?"

I shook my head. "They're unregistered. They all have ghost tags."

"Weird," he said. He started eating the Combos again. I counted six and then he added, "You know what else is weird? How fast they found us at all. You only saw that alert last night, right?"

"Right."

"And that server is physically in Utah?"

"New Jersey."

"Even further. That doesn't strike you as strange?"

Of course it struck me as strange. I'd been thinking about it since I realized those guys at work were specifically there for me and Thom. How in the world had they identified and located us so quickly? It should take more than a few hours for a remote online threat to become an in-person, in-the-room, pursuing-you-in-a-suit menace.

"I'm missing something," I told him. "They know too much about us, whoever they are."

Thom returned to his Combos. He was going to stress-eat the whole bag. It was his version of being quiet to let me think, so I tried to ignore the faux-peroni smell and stale munching noises. I tried, in fact, to think. We drove the next hour without speaking.

12

MIKE

THE STREET WHERE SHE LIVED

'd spent five years installing and upgrading surveillance in Ruth's apartment, never imagining having to disassemble it piece by expensive piece while she drove away from me at sixty-seven miles an hour. Multiple cameras and microphones captured every angle and corner of the living room and the kitchen. I could feel the men watching. I could imagine their comments as I went to remove equipment first from the bathroom, then from the bedroom. If they had wondered whether this was a legal operation, they knew now it was not. Their judgment didn't shame me. Did Manet consult the brush-wash boy while he painted *Olympia*?

I'd followed her nearly full time for seven years, her voice and image streaming to my computer monitor or to my iPhone. I'd watched her while I cooked dinner, sometimes lecturing her unlistening self on the value of phytochemicals and roughage. She'd sat next to me on the couch at night, working on her laptop while I watched TV. She'd need to learn some balance, or she'd burn out by thirty. I developed a habit of talking to her, even though I knew she couldn't answer directly. I did it deliberately, to maintain respect for her humanity. It would have been too easy to treat her merely as an asset.

Ruth had become my primary companion—her face the last thing I saw before sleep, and my welcome first sight every morning. It hurt to take down the cameras. I blamed her for that a little, for leaving, though it was arguably me who had triggered that. My screwdriver slipped, and I stripped the set screw in an outlet plate. I was not my normal patient self.

"I don't suppose anyone thought to bring real tools?" I asked the room. Which was pure temper, because I was the official thinker in the group, and this was my operation. I was using the tiny half-useless repair kit that rode under the seat of the Agency SUV. It had probably come with the vehicle. My men exchanged glances and didn't answer. They were leafing through the books, checking every shelf and drawer, flexing the floorboards, looking for documentation of the missing puzzle pieces in Ruth's great hack. I knew they wouldn't find anything. I knew but they had to look anyhow. The specific series of hidden gates in that chip and how to access them? She would have committed that to memory and destroyed the original design. It was find Ruth and convince her to talk, or bribe a couple of dinosaur electrical engineers off their retirement yachts and sheep farms, then lock them in a room for a year to do gate-by-gate analysis and hope they uncovered it.

I counted to five and exhaled slowly. This was the wrong way to be spending the first hour after Ruth blew cover and ran. Of course I could find her anytime, but so could anyone or anything else. She might get hit by a truck, bit by a rabid squirrel, crushed by a meteorite. Nevertheless, I had to balance her protection against the national interest. Most of the cameras and microphones were technically experimental. I'd borrowed them from our lab for a fake operational field test; that protocol allowed me to monitor a US citizen on US soil indefinitely without a warrant. It would be damaging if a random person stumbled across my equipment and decided to talk about it. In Menlo Park, with my luck, it would be a technically savvy Instagram influencer or similar nightmare. Also, I couldn't rule out some other entity having noticed Ruth. In the years of supervising her, guiding her from afar, what were the odds that a hostile power had identified her? I needed to recover my gear in case someone else came looking. I could leave a man to watch the apartment. Ruth would never come back, but another party might tip their hand.

"Boss." It was Earl. He was holding the violin in one hand, pulling a rippled piece of paper from the lining of the case: a white page with blue printing.

I grabbed it. I hadn't known about this. A puzzle piece for sure.

"Neptune Oyster," I read. I held the menu to the light.

Several entries were faintly starred in pencil. "Chatham Blue Mussels, seventeen," I continued. "Indooja, what is that? Indooja Calabrese, basil, toasted garlic. Also Black Bass, seventeen, pomegranate, finger lime, lava sea salt. And Scarlet Prawn Mozambique, forty-one, Camargue red rice, azafran? Brussels sprouts, pea shoots!" This was a huge and unexpected break. I looked around the room. "What do you guys notice about that? What jumps out?"

Earl said, "I notice it's all seafood. So maybe she likes seafood?"

I snorted. "Oh hell no. She doesn't care about food. The prices are all prime numbers. Obviously. Seventeen, seventeen, forty-one? All prime." I waved the menu triumphantly. "It's a cryptographic key. A key hidden in a menu."

13

RUTH

HOW I LEARNED
TO ROB BANKS

'd turned east on 4, then north on 160, and was starting to work our way toward Reno. I'd forgotten about the toll-booths, which meant cameras, and I was fighting full linear panic. Also I was getting hungry. Thom was doing loud origami with the Combos bag. I forced my thoughts into order. A couple of things now seemed obvious, and I've found that obvious things, especially the nasty unexpected ones, are usually true. Obvious Thing 1: those guys could not have found us in a couple of hours, so they'd been onto us before this morning. Obvious Thing 2: they could not have located my apartment in the few minutes it took them to drive to it, so they'd known about that already too. And the most likely way they'd found my home was that I had led them to it. So they hadn't just found me, they had already been there, maybe listening, probably watching. How long had that been true?

This line of thinking led me back to the man in the suit who'd waved in the Ops Center. He either looked like Hydrant Mike, which was an ordinary coincidence in a zip code with a rich harvest of expensively suited sagging white guys, but left the weird familiarity unexplained. Or he was the real Hydrant Mike, which was a horrible thought, but in my nightmare alternate universe might also be the obvious one.

It was true what I'd told Thom: that Hydrant Mike had been a sales guy at my last company. It was also true that the CEO's antique microdog had pissed his shoes at a party. That's not why he mattered. Hydrant Mike had been the unwitting catalyst for the single major insight that had coalesced my plan. He'd booked the customer visit, forced me to attend it, driven the car.

After I'd found the router problem, I decided to get a job in microchip product management. I knew the data sensitivity I'd found was a glitch. I was interested that it hadn't shown up in testing, and I was more curious whether there was a way to introduce other behaviors that weren't bugs, but were undocumented. I still didn't know what I was looking for, exactly, but I'd caught the scent of money.

I could never be undereducated and make a good life thieving. The people paid to stop me have stood guard for a long time, usually. They know their one thing (or their seven things) really well. So I need to understand those things better than they do, and everything around those things as well. That's how to find a way in and out without jail time. The best thieves are lifelong students. So I'd taken classes in microchip design, formally and socially. Then I'd applied for a product management job at a smaller chip company in Silicon Valley, one that lacked the infrastructure to audit its development processes. My background building and troubleshooting real networks got me through the door. The initial formal job description was to identify product revenue opportunities in small and midsize businesses. I may have mentioned in my interview that I particularly liked banks.

I'd learned right away that many small and medium banks conducted business on ancient computer crap heaps. Decrepit custom software limped along on twenty-year-old hardware. They couldn't afford to update their systems or to disclose how shitty they were. Propping up the daily business absorbed their staff; no one was available or qualified to move their operations onto modern commercial software that could run on newer hardware. It was like popping the hood on a late-model SUV and finding a trio of scrofulous hamsters powering the serpentine belt, fighting over a moldy raisin. As transactions had been forced online, these banks had started hiding their ugly servers behind firewalls, hoping to get away with it. It was an obvious opportunity for my new employer to build a chip that went onto a card that went into a firewall to shield these fragile and temperamental hunks of junk; it was simpler and cheaper than what they could cobble together on their own, and they could outsource the management and monitoring. For me, it put heaps of poorly protected money within reach. My new job was a natural next step.

Mike (Hydrant Mike, in his pre-pissed-on incarnation) was in charge of selling our chips to the companies that built those network routers. He was a channel sales representative, which is a strange role in any technology company. Channel sales, where you sell to an intermediary that resells in volume to downstream customers, provides crucial revenue. There's a huge potential multiplier to any success, and the cost of fulfilling and supporting any sale is generally low. That's the upside, and it makes those guys important. But that same math significantly amplifies any bullshit, deliberate or otherwise, which means channel reps can seem far stupider than other salespeople. Since they almost never meet the end customer, they also tend to get lazier over time. They can plug a thousand toilets in one go, then delegate the plunger. Channel sales reps are rarely popular.

But they have sway. They like to drag actual productive people along on their calls, to cover their ignorance and flaunt their status in the corporate hierarchy. Mike was known for this behavior, so it wasn't a shock when my boss came to my cubicle, Mike in tow, and announced I'd been assigned to go along on several very important customer pitches. My boss looked a little embarrassed to be wasting my time; Pre-Hydrant Mike just stood, smirking.

And he was an irritating companion. If it had occurred to me to pee on his shoes, I might have done it. As it was, I practiced shutting down his overly familiar chitchat and smarmy shared-mission shtick. Also the convention for these coerced sales support calls was to buy your hostage a good lunch, but Mike never stopped for food at all. He was the birdbook entry for channel sales: a self-important jerk. Anyhow, the priority visit was the last in a long day. We went to one of the large router manufacturers (not my ultimate employer), and found ourselves presenting to a slightly random group of other sales people and senior technical staff. The conversation eventually turned to pricing structure and volume discounts. Mike turned to me and, in a flash of humanity, said, "You can skip this part if you want. Check your email or whatever. Just meet me back at the car in an hour."

I was surprised. "They won't mind?"

He shook his head. "They won't care. Take a break."

I picked up my bag and fled the room. The parking lot was a right turn, so I took a left and wandered off to explore the building. There were restrooms, a few small meeting rooms (empty), and then I went through two sets of double doors, around a corner, down some stairs, through a bright blue door, and found myself in a large, packed lab. There were racks of equipment, wires everywhere, a soldering iron, a microscope, lots of small tools, and a bonanza of red fire extinguishers. And there were three guys completely absorbed in whatever they were doing: one at a keyboard, the second looking over his shoulder, and the third laying a smartphone out on a yellow fiberglass welding blanket.

They didn't acknowledge my entrance. The hovering guy said something to the keyboard guy; the one with the phone stepped back and picked up a fire extinguisher. Keyboard Guy started typing, hit enter, and looked over his shoulder as the smartphone rebooted, started to smoke, and caught fire. Everyone laughed madly (a sure tell for an engineer, by the way: that wild laugh when valuable things fail dangerously); the one with the fire extinguisher pulled the trigger before the lithium battery could explode, and then all three of them turned to face me.

"Um, hi," I said. I had no plausible reason to be in their lab, so I didn't offer one. "What did you guys just do?"

They looked at each other. Then Keyboard Guy tipped his head. "Come here. I'll show you."

I went and stood by the screen. He was using a software packet editor to fabricate and inject traffic onto the local Wi-Fi network. I recognized the program—we used to use those things all the time for monitoring, testing, even forcing updates in network routing tables.

"So you're fabricating specific packets that target that phone," I said. I bent closer. "I don't recognize that destination port, though, or the format." I looked at him. "Obviously you found a hot spot. What am I looking at? Is that a custom phone?"

"Stock phone." He rolled his chair back from the table. "How much do you know about microchip design?"

I shrugged. "Just enough to get through some of the high-level stuff. We develop the specification for a custom chip and send it to the fabricator. So I know enough to stay within design and budget limits." I sat down on the edge of the table. "I haven't graduated to pyrotechnics."

He laughed. The others moved to join the conversation. I set down my bag. There are moments that matter more than others in life. I miss most of them. But in that lab, the air was vibrating with a crazy secret energy, and something inside me caught the rhythm. I felt seen but had no urge to hide. This was not my tribe—I have no tribe—but fellow travelers, maybe, teachers, and, very briefly, friends.

Fire Extinguisher Guy pushed his sleeves up. "So what's the qualification process, when you get the prototype back from the fabricator?"

"Well, we work from the original spec and generate functional tests to make sure the chip performs as we expect, and within tolerances."

"And if it does?"

"Then we accept it, order a production run."

Keyboard Guy had been spinning around and around in his chair. He stopped. "So if they leave something out, you'll know."

I nodded. "Sure. If the tests are complete."

"And"—he watched my face—"if someone adds something else to your chip, something extra, something undocumented. How do you find that?"

Silence. Him waiting for me, and me schooling my face, my hands, my whole self to stillness because I saw at once, and in its full beauty, the shape of my plan. I could smell, taste, feel money. A lot of money. Maybe that's a human thing, or maybe it's special to thieves, but I was immersed in the sudden comprehension of my fortune-to-be, not yet stolen but suddenly tangible, and in reach. I would hide a backdoor in a firewall microchip. I would break into the flimsy bank servers behind it to carry off small amounts of digital money. I would be so rich, eventually. I met his gaze. "You don't find it. Not without a gate-by-gate analysis or total luck capturing the exploit in action. It's nearly impossible."

The guys all smiled. "Exactly," said Keyboard Guy. "That's where we come in. We look for those things, try to figure them out." He rolled back to the keyboard. "It's still pretty brute-force. We generate a ton of traffic addressing the chip against a range of possible ports and monitor the chip for any interesting state change."

"But—" I said, then stopped.

"But?"

I shook my head. "No, nothing. I get it. I see the limits of that approach, but so do you. I can't tell you how to do it better."

"Show her the biometric one." This was Watching-over-the-Shoulder Guy, who had been listening quietly. There was some silent group calculation, and then Keyboard Guy nodded assent.

"Sure. It's a good one." He looked at me. "This hack isn't network based." He pulled an iPad off the shelf, opened the settings. He unlocked it and went to the Touch ID & Passcode section. "I want you to see that the fingerprint authentication is completely turned off." He showed me, and it was—no stored fingerprints, no Touch ID requirement. "Now look," he said, and locked the tablet. Watching-over-the-Shoulder Guy fished in his pocket and pulled out a purple plastic finger on a key ring. They'd decorated it with a Dora the Explorer Band-Aid and nail polish. He turned it so I could see the swirl of a very specific and completely unnatural scrolled pattern on the fingertip. He held the patterned side against the iPad thumbprint reader, adjusted its position, and the screen unlocked.

"Shit." I looked at him. "They all do that?"

"All the ones we've tested." Watching-over-the-Shoulder Guy put the finger back in his pocket.

"Just that specific pattern?"

"As far as we know."

"You did not just stumble on that by chance."

He smiled. "Correct. We did not." He took the iPad and set it carefully on the shelf. Turned back. "I'm Gideon. These two bozos"—he indicated Keyboard Guy and Fire Extinguisher Guy—"are Josh and Sam."

"Ruth," I told them.

"Ah," said Sam. "As in, 'Entreat me not to leave thee, or to turn back from following after thee . . .'" It was Old Testament, the book of Ruth, her famous, pathetic plea of devotion to her mother-in-law, Naomi, where she vows to trade her body for a new home and to belong somewhere. Also where she proves her willingness to do anything not to return to her blood family, but no one talks about that.

"Yes," I answered, "but also no." My phone vibrated. A text told me Mike was at the car and I was not. "I have to go." I picked up my bag. "This was . . . enlightening. Thank you, guys. Thank you so much."

Gideon followed me to the door. As I reached for it, he said, "Ruth." I turned. He handed me a card with a handwritten phone number. "Keep this. I'm not creeping on you. Just take it. If you get in trouble, call me." I stared at him.

"I'm serious," he said. "I'm that guy. People bring me stuff. Problems, solutions, a bit of everything."

I took the card. "Silicone thumbs?"

"Sometimes." His eyes were very dark. "If you need help someday, don't even think about it. Call me."

"What kind of help?" I asked him.

"You'll know it when you need it." He grinned at me. I tucked the card in my pocket and went to meet Pre-Hydrant Mike. I wondered what else was in Gideon's pockets. And no surprise, I held on to that card.

14

MIKE

AENEAS DIDN'T FILE EXPENSE REPORTS

We cleared the apartment, and then I took my crew back to the hotel to retrieve luggage, and to change into dry clothes. After that slow process, they wanted lunch. So often, I find myself babysitting while my real work waits undone. But wet men are whiny, and hungry men are stupid. Ruth and Thom had been soaked by the same sprinklers—I didn't see her stopping for a meatball sub or to refresh her wardrobe. But my team took priority. Institutional service often devolves into satisfying the desires of the men we're called to lead, and the men we're obliged to follow. When I was a little boy, I'd loved heroes. I'd memorized long sections of *The Aeneid*; I'd fantasized about difficult journeys and tragic choices. And in a complex way, I'd grown into the man I'd hoped to become. It's hard for most people to recognize that the signifiers of heroism have evolved with human progress. When Aeneas managed up, he was pleading with Juno. Now a man who would have carried a sword sends an email and briefs his boss. He buys sandwiches for his men with his corporate card. The glory is obscured, but it remains glory.

I left my team eating and took my sandwich to my room. I photographed the coded menu and sent pictures on a secure line to our cryptographers. I was anxious to get back on the road. A million times, I'd considered the impending encounter. I was confident she'd come to me willingly when we met again, face-to-face. By now, she would have put together my role in her story. She would have remembered it was I who delivered her to that lab. She should have intuited my benevolent presence in the years that followed. If there'd been a way to leave the hotel and pursue her on my own, I'd have chosen it. Protocol mattered, however, and there was a chance that Ruth would make another mistake. It had certainly been her day for it.

It was 1400 hours before we got back onto the road. I dropped one man back to keep an eye on Ruth's apartment, and then we headed to the highway, Earl driving and me beside him, watching the livestream and navigating. Ruth and Thom were coming into Sacramento, not speaking. Thom was playing with a snack bag. Ruth looked grim. She was wearing a blond wig, not quite her color—it washed her out. I wondered if I'd missed an argument. They merged onto I-80, and then Ruth was taking the exit. Thom opened his mouth to speak.

Ruth cut her head sharply. She raised her hand, demanding silence. Finally, she was sick of Thom. That made both of us.

Ruth pulled into a Walmart parking lot. She took out her pad and wrote something while Thom looked over her shoulder. Then they both got out and headed into the store. They split up without a word.

It was overconfident, I thought, to stop for shopping. Our lunch delay wouldn't matter after all. Ruth was delivering herself nicely to us. But her list puzzled me. I watched her select a new (and unflattering) outfit, including shoes. It seemed reasonable, given her morning soaking. Then she picked out new versions of everything in her bag, except the money. When she met Thom at the register, he also had a full set of clothes. They checked out in silence, paid with cash, and went to the restrooms behind the register. Ruth changed down to the skin. Then she dumped everything from her bag into the trash, replacing it with her new purchases. Thom was waiting for her, also wearing his new clothes. He looked at her, and then he shook his head. He signaled for her to wait, and ran back to the checkout. In a minute, he returned, carrying a reusable shopping bag. It was absurdly ugly, covered in dancing fruit. He handed it to her. Silently Ruth took her shoulder bag, the one she'd stolen to celebrate her first paycheck after college, the single thing she'd carried everywhere since, and dumped its contents into the shopping bag. She walked back into the women's restroom and shoved the empty shoulder bag, including the tiny cameras, microphones, and GPS trackers—all embedded in the strap and the trim rivets—into the overflowing trash can.

She threw me in the trash, and she walked away. Maybe she pranced or flew, I couldn't see to tell you. She left that restroom, and I sat in the front passenger seat of the SUV, chasing her north, staring at used feminine products, and listening to Walmart radio. For the first time in seven years, I didn't know where she was. I was alone.

15

RUTH

A PLAGUE OF BUGS

It took me too long, but I got there. Something, maybe everything I owned, had to be bugged. Probably the fucking car too. Because why peel off to search my apartment unless they knew they could find us again? That apartment wasn't going anywhere. The only thing to do was stop talking and replace everything. After we bought our new things (and I was so upset, I forgot snacks), we sat outside at one of those depressing Walmart picnic tables. I'd always wondered what sorry desperadoes used them. Now I knew. The tables existed to serve fleeing international bank robbers. There was a camera pointed straight at us, probably to oppress the employees who took smoke breaks there. The lens was shattered, I hoped by those same employees, so it seemed low risk.

I was strangely sad about losing my wig. It had been real hair. I'd left it by the baby changing station, hoping a blond cancer patient might find it. I handed Thom one of the new burners. I'd managed not to pay for those, a small morale builder.

I asked, "What do you think about calling Toby and giving him your Apple ID login? Maybe he can check on that AirTag for us."

"Do you think they know where we are right now?"

I shrugged. "Probably. If we had bugs on us, they tracked them, at least, to those restrooms. The thing I don't know about is the car. I can't decide if we need to ditch it now or not." That's what I said. But we both knew that running in a known car was pointless. And they probably could ID the plate, even if they hadn't bugged the interior. "Just call Toby."

Thom dialed. "Hey, sweetie," I heard him say. "No, it's OK. It's a new phone."

I walked away to let them talk. A small grassy slope bordered the asphalt. I found a bench and sat down, disturbing a pair of pigeons who were picking through the scattered paper trash. It was actually a pretty day for the Central Valley. The sunshine was gentle, and there were a few fluffy clouds pinned to a very blue sky. We still hadn't talked about Thom's plan to turn himself in. I was still hungry. We were in a Sacramento Walmart parking lot without transportation. There was nowhere certain to go after I solved that problem. The guy who might be Hydrant Mike was slithering up the highway behind us for unknown but obviously malevolent reasons. I had a lot of problems for a gajillionaire.

16

MIKE

FATED

When people first met Ruth, they'd call her smart, maybe the smartest girl they knew. When they heard what she'd done, they'd call her a criminal. But to describe her either way was to miss the point. She was smart like that x-radiograph machine was smart when they directed it at Van Gogh's shoes and found flowers underneath. What I pointed her toward, she saw through immediately. One might ask, Where lies the intelligence? Is it in the art expert, or in the machine? I can affirm that ours was a shared genius. And Ruth was a criminal like a river at flood stage is a criminal when it carries valuables away. You can shake your finger, if you choose, but you're wiser to dredge the channel. My Ruth was a wounded heart longing for refuge. She took money because she couldn't imagine a safer shelter. In other words, because she didn't know me.

Ruth dressed badly; she pushed up her sleeves, even in a suit jacket. She was kind to animals. But the main thing was, she was always some kind of thief, specifically the kind that steals things and doesn't get caught. And a thief that doesn't get caught, especially a sharp, pretty one who feels invincible, well, she can get ambitious. How could she know that the whole time she was devising and executing her heist, it was I who held her, safe in the palm of my hand. I found her before she knew someone might be looking. She might as well have tried to hide from the sky.

Ruth attended a university where my agency does some recruiting. Our process is useful for enlisting certain types of young people: the flaming patriots, needy aspiring bureaucrats, niche intellectual obsessives who want a salary to excel in obscure languages, and a certain soldierly temperament that aspires to a battle with great existential stakes. That last category is where I'd place myself, of course. There's an additional type that is arguably rarest and most valuable, but is also, on the face of it, unrecruitable. Ruth was one such individual—an almost pathologically nonconformist spirit, best handled from a distance, behind an impenetrable veil of environmental camouflage.

I was in an ideal stage of life to engage her. I was newly forty, perpetually single, and I had watched mediocre colleagues succeed well beyond their merits, leaving me to struggle on in skeptical subservience. I was too meticulous, too committed to the good of the nation, and too mindful of my own integrity to choose an easy path of professional accolades. "Remarkable for righteousness and service," like Virgil's Aeneas, I'm proof a modern man can have talent and advantages, yet not exploit them to satisfy his own vanity or to accrue the external trappings of success. I still believe the rewards that come with age and long effort are most authentic and durable. You could say I was a seeker at the time, searching for something different, difficult, and worthy of my commitment. Virgil said it: "Fate had made [me] fugitive." I longed for a personal mission of service to my country, then I discovered Ruth.

I was in the administrative offices, reviewing the financial records for potential candidates. Specifically, I was looking at delinquent payments, since those individuals are often alert to the value of Agency support. There were seventeen accounts at risk of financial suspension. As I scrolled through them, the system crashed and failed to reboot.

"No worries," said the woman assisting me. "We have wonderful technical support. They'll have us back up in no time, I'm sure."

A technician arrived promptly, sat down at the console, and began her troubleshooting. I noticed she was a young woman, likely a student, attractive but averse to display. She did not speak or make eye contact. In fact, she never seemed to notice us. In less than fifteen minutes, she had the system back online and even reopened the financial database to our previous view. I returned to my chair and saw sixteen accounts delinquent. It was my moment of inspiration. That technician had restored the software and updated her own tuition status at the same time. Quite likely, she had remotely initiated the original failure purely to modify her account. I scanned the room, but she'd left. No matter. At some point in my visit, I would seize the opportunity to find her again, learn her name, install a camera in her bag.

Of course I might have approached her directly, tried to pressure her with my knowledge of her actions. I sensed that would not be productive. A girl like that would simply vanish and start over elsewhere. And what did I care how she accounted for her schooling? Remember that Dido, tragic fallen queen of *The Aeneid*, funded the founding of Carthage with treasure buried by someone else. I also never reported Ruth's acquisition as an asset. Her surveillance was always covered as equipment testing. What had I seen, after all? A girl removed a database entry, and my world shifted. I needed time to incubate that raw talent, the mind that would rearrange the technical world to enable her own silent ascent. With minimal guidance, I believed Ruth would show me things that a willing volunteer would never find. She was nineteen when I first saw her. I have been her mentor, her protector, her watcher, and her warmest admirer ever since.

17

RUTH

WAITING FOR ENLIGHTENMENT IN A WALMART PARKING LOT

I n my early twenties, I had a phase of collecting menus. It was aspirational, I suppose, the way certain boys collect car photos or pornography. I had some good ones: the Musket Room, Neptune Oyster, La Frontera. Insomniac nights when loneliness struck, I'd pull them out, place imaginary orders, try to visualize a great meal that might wait down along the peculiar path I was bushwhacking. Eventually I threw them away. I realized that anything I relied on for comfort could become a crutch, a weakness that might muddle my clarity or delay a decision when I most needed to move quickly and dispassionately. Sentiment is always an enemy, no matter how harmless its object may seem.

Thom, for example. I should not have brought him in. I should have improved my own scripting. But I'd grown lazy and let my impatience win. And Thom had been easy to recruit. He was a guy who'd take a dropped dollar to the lost and found, but also claim the pot after cheating at the office pool.

I'd done the most difficult technical piece alone—I'd inserted an undocumented function into our new microchip that allowed me secret, silent access through any device that contained that chip. It was a door through the firewall that only I knew how to find and open. I'd designed the chip, had it fabricated, then deleted and falsified the functional specification. In my apartment, alone, I'd tested my access. And creepy Hydrant Mike (well pissed on by then) had driven that chip through the channel: hundreds of them, all over the internet, quite a few protecting vulnerable bank servers. I'd changed jobs and companies so I could scout those banks directly. The largest reseller of my new chip had been glad to hire me. All that remained was to recruit someone to help build a simple software system that logged into those servers through my backdoor. We'd hacked each server and created a small bogus account; every few nights, those fake accounts made an inconspicuous transfer through our system into an offshore account. Well, several offshore accounts, as I've said. Once Thom had written the original scripts, I'd deployed a second network that funneled cash to my other accounts. He never knew about that, just like he didn't know precisely how we got through the firewalls.

So I'd been in a hurry, or lonely; anyhow, I'd brought Thom on board, and now I was sitting in that Sacramento parking lot waiting helplessly for Mike or someone Mike-like to come, I don't know, execute us? Imprison us? Take us to the local Golden Corral buffet and drown us in the chocolate fountain? Whatever fate this Maybe-Mike intended for me, it felt a long way from the luxury I'd anticipated.

Thom sat down on the other end of the bench. "Toby says that AirTag crossed the Dumbarton Bridge and took 880 to 80. They're about an hour away." He was fidgeting and looked scared.

I said, "So they're definitely not police."

Thom looked unsure.

"Think about it. If they were, we'd be crawling with local cops right now. They obviously know we came to Sacramento. This feels more like *Spy vs Spy* than cops and robbers."

Thom replied, "I guess they aren't Mafia either—they didn't shoot us in the Ops Center."

I hadn't thought of Mafia. "I guess Mafia might have sprung for a second car waiting outside. Whoever they are, they don't represent our worldwide fan club." I tucked up a leg and turned to face him. "Look, Thom, what's your plan? Are you really wanting to turn yourself in? Because I still think we can both get away. You can go somewhere. Toby can join you. You guys will have enough money to do whatever."

Thom looked at the ground. He dug a little hole in the dirt

with the toe of his bright new Walmart sneaker. "It's not that simple."

"The details need work, but it actually does seem that simple to me."

"No," he said. "It's not." And then he told me about the cash in his mattress. It turned out he'd been pilfering funds from the Caymans account for over a year. He'd been withdrawing cash and hiding it in his actual mattress. Because no one would think to check that. All day, Thom had been planning to rat me out, to trade immunity and a chance to abscond with his stash for his pathetic partial understanding of my heist. It's a persistent blind spot of mine, expecting reciprocity. I'd paid him millions. That should have bought some loyalty.

I heard him out on his self-inflicted problem. It's a manners paradox when a person tells you he's done something totally stupid. Because it's rude to say so, even though (to me) pretending the dumb thing was normal implies more judgment. So I stared at him. Talk about a rookie fuckup. It's not stealing if you can't get away—the term for that is getting caught. He'd pulled a Winnie the Pooh, wedged in his own doorway.

"Well," I said finally, "that's a problem. They for sure have your address. Do you even know the money is still there?"

He shrugged defensively. "Toby says they haven't been to my place."

"Toby's there?"

"He was parked across the street. I sent him to check. He knows about the money."

There's no point restating that Thom was one of my mistakes.

I sighed. "Well, that's interesting. I guess they're focused on finding us."

Thom shifted on the bench. "Finding *you*. Toby and I think they're really after you, not me."

He was probably right, but his tone was aggravating. I imagined kicking him hard. I imagined him flat beneath a cartoon anvil. I imagined sitting on that anvil in the sunshine, swinging my legs and eating a caprese panini with extra basil, letting the oil drip down onto his flattened face. "Well, you can test that theory. You could go sit in the car over there, ask them for a ride when they show up."

Thom didn't answer.

"OK, fine, what do you want to do? You want to call an Uber and go home? They'll get there, but maybe not right away. You might have time to close your mattress account and blow town."

He said, defiantly, "Toby's coming to get me. We're going back together for the money."

I hoped I never had to rely on Thom again. "How far out is he?"

"Just over an hour. He's behind that black SUV."

"He's meeting us here?"

Thom stared at his dirty sneaker toe. "Me," he muttered. "He's meeting *me* here."

"Thom," I said. "For fuck's sake. We aren't wearing wolf

collars. They're tracking the car, or something we left in the trash. They absolutely are not tracking us."

"What if they somehow microchipped you?"

I laughed. "I think I'd remember that needle."

He didn't look persuaded.

"OK. What if they did? Where's the transmitter? Where's the power source? Even if I am microchipped, which I'm not, they'd have to find me, immobilize me, scan me with a reader. It wouldn't lead them to me. Just think about it, Thom. You're an engineer."

"I guess so," he said, "but I still think we should split up."

"Yes," I said. "All right." I bit my tongue for a moment. He wasn't wrong. It was possible he and Toby could get clear away, dragging their lumpy mattress. I had no urge to help with that project. I could disappear more easily alone. My resistance was irrational, a fantasy grasping back to the buddy phase of this theft, obviously well past. "Would you guys give me a lift just back to that truck stop on 80? Please?"

Thom sighed. "I guess so," he said.

I did not slap him. I didn't offer him $25 million, approximately the amount he'd stashed in his mattress, his half (he thought) of the heist money. I smiled. "Thank you." I stretched my legs. "Let's get food and a pair of binoculars. I want a closer look at that guy in the suit."

We went back into the store. Then we sat on the dirt in the sun where we could watch the entrance. We picked the plastic off our mushy sandwiches. Thom was in a good mood. It cheered him to know he was going to be rid of me.

"Remember that shaved ice on Grand Cayman? I want to take Toby back there."

I thought about no-fly lists and Thom and Toby questioned separately in tiny rooms. "Yeah," I said. "It was really good. I liked the place that did the coffee one."

I was tossing damp twists of bread to the pigeons when the black SUV rolled up to the store entrance. I looked through my binoculars. Familiar Docker guy driving, and yes, there was Hydrant Mike in the passenger seat—not his look-alike, but the actual guy. I had no clue what it meant, but it wasn't good. I watched them rush importantly into the store, leaving the SUV right in the crosswalk. I hate when people do that.

"I bet they left it running," I said.

"What?" said Thom. "Oh no. No. Do not. No."

"Hold my binoculars," I said, and speed-walked toward the SUV.

They had indeed left it running in front of the entrance, with the dongle on the console. I only meant to take the dongle. Then I saw my father's violin in the back, with Thom's backpack and windbreaker. Those damn thieves. I slid into the driver's seat, drove the SUV around back to the loading dock, and pulled it out of sight between two dumpsters. It made no sense to reclaim our stuff, but I tried for a moment to think of a way. I'm not musical, but I'd carried that violin with me for years. I'd thought it would help me remember him, but it had not. He was vapor in my mind. There'd been a song I thought he'd played me, "The Mountain House." I'd listened to it from time to time, trying to stir a feeling I hoped I'd felt with him.

One day, I'd googled and learned it was written long after he'd gone. Now I touched the case and felt nothing. Mike could have it. Escape would be my father's legacy; he'd excelled at that.

I shut off the engine and locked the doors. I tossed the dongle in a dumpster and walked back to Thom. The whole thing took a few minutes. I didn't get caught. I felt better. It was worth it.

"You're insane," said Thom, and then he started to giggle.

We were both laughing when Toby pulled up, rolled down his window, and told us to get in. A minute later, we were headed south on 80.

They dropped me at the 49er Travel Plaza on the west side of Sacramento. Toby started to argue the decision—I could see he wanted a third person on the mattress job—but he caught a look from Thom. "OK," he said. "Be careful, I guess."

I hugged him through the window. Waved at Thom. "You guys be safe, and send me an email. I'll see it somehow." I was ready to not deal with Thom. I stepped back and watched them go.

18

MIKE

DAMN SACRAMENTO

It was a mistake to drive on to Sacramento. I might have reconsidered, if I hadn't been distracted defending my choices to Earl. Sure, he happened to call that one thing right. It was a lucky guess for a management consultant with less than a month's tenure on my project. I had seven years in, and Ruth should have done what I expected her to do, which was to wait for me by that Walmart. Maybe she would have, if I'd come alone. Instead I chased her with a gang of yahoos, and she did what she should not have, even though Earl predicted it. She disappeared.

I hadn't put trackers on the cars. I'd recorded the plates, but Ruth had been so attached to that bag. Ditching it was unexpected. Of course it was a hassle to retrieve her things from the women's room. I'm sure she intended that as a commentary on my all-male team. It would be easy for a person who didn't know me or Ruth to misconstrue her as my victim, but through the years, she'd found her ways to critique my process. I know that, on some level, she consented to my presence, and accepted my counsel. This assertion seems fantastic, but I had proof. After Ruth moved to California, for example, she'd indulged an alarming phase of promiscuity. I allowed it, for a time; she was young and lacked role models. When my tolerance wore thin, however, she sensed it, and she stopped. Our communication went both ways, always.

In that Walmart, she forced us to find a supervisor, who found a manager, who called a senior manager, just to retrieve the trash bag. They said we'd need a warrant to close the restroom for a search. In the end, I sat on a bench by the parking lot, picking through the damp horror of women's restroom trash. A nasty process but, as I observed to Earl, worthwhile. Not only did I retrieve Ruth's bag and its fortune in cameras, trackers, and microphones, I realized at last that I hadn't recovered the wig. I told Earl, trying not be smug, "Now we know she's still wearing that wig. We're looking for a blond." A washed-out vanished blond, unfortunately.

We sat for a moment surrounded by rubbish. Then Earl said, "Boss, I think it's time to run this whole thing up the flagpole." By which he meant, it was time for me to confess my program to my boss at the Agency or he would turn me in.

"OK," I said. "You win." And then I looked around. "Where'd you park the SUV?"

Sacramento is such a cesspool. We left that SUV for twenty

minutes, if that, and it got stolen. They found it around back eventually, nothing taken but the dongle. That incident cost us two hours. And it made me look particularly stupid, calling for a lift after losing my vehicle and the high-value, minimally documented asset I'd been chasing in it.

"At least we kept our pants!" said Earl. He thought it was funny. "Bet it was her," he told me as we rode to San Francisco in the back seat of an Agency sedan. "She made you, sir."

I held my tongue. Like every consultant, he had some useful skills (though he was now fired as my driver), but he did not understand Ruth.

He stared out the window. "Wonder if we're driving right past them," he said. "She probably went straight to ground somewhere nearby."

I couldn't take it. "She's not still local. We surprised her, and she panicked," I told him. "I think she took a chance on that car. She'll be at the Canadian frontier in Oroville, Washington, in twelve hours, give or take. I'm sure of it. Just her. She'll have dumped Thom somewhere, you can count on that."

Earl was not convinced. "Why would she go to Canada?" he asked. "There's literally no point going there. She's smarter than that. She must know we'd be watching the borders."

"Pointless is the whole point," I said, not like I owed him the insight. North she had bolted, and north she would continue, because I was not there to steer. I knew I needed a different reason for Earl. "It's where people go when they plan to come back. She's proving she can leave if she wants to. She's negotiating with me."

"Sounds complicated," said Earl. He smirked. "My chips are on the not-Canada pocket."

He annoyed me, but he also didn't matter, so I let it drop and concentrated on how I was going to brief my boss. Unfortunately, my grand unveiling was going to be clouded by Ruth's recent unforced errors. It would not be an easy conversation.

19

RUTH

YOU CAN FIND ANYTHING AT A GOOD TRUCK STOP

I like truck stops. They aren't quite their own countries, but they have an autonomous quality, like a mini Texas or a lesser Star Wars planet, with fewer bar fights. This one had cameras, and I dawdled awhile by the ice machine, trying to think of some clever way to disable them. It didn't seem like the moment to improvise with electrical boxes. Wherever those images went, I knew it wasn't to some organized central repository where stone-faced seekers scanned the footage with terrible efficiency. If my pursuers tracked me from these cameras, it would take a direct tip. The people here were the threat if they saw a photo and recognized me. Fortunately they all saw hundreds of people a day, and as I've said, I'm not memorable.

I paid cash for a single room; the cashier didn't look up. I found it and locked the door behind me. In a movie, this step would have initiated the hair-cutting-and-dyeing disguise montage, but I was reluctant to do anything that made anyone scrutinize me or my photo ID. Maybe I was hoping the fuss would blow over. Nothing outlasts a bad haircut, I decided, not even a villainous pursuit. The room smelled of industrial cleaner, with a persistent base note of mildew that I couldn't localize to any specific item or corner. The sunlight was starting to fade. I sat down on the bed to think.

I had new information since last night. My situation seemed worse than I'd imagined. What if, years ago, Hydrant Mike had learned about my visit to the lab? What if he or someone else had deduced I'd hidden functions in that network chip? If he'd been a real salesman back then (certainly he'd been selling things), he had a side gig now that involved chasing me. Silicon Valley was rotten with low-level spooks. What if he'd been a government flunky all along? If I let that story be true, I had two immediate extra-credit questions: Why had they let me run so far for so long, and why were they chasing me now? The men I'd seen today hadn't struck me as the varsity squad, so the decision-makers must be elsewhere. What did they want?

I stepped through the facts I had, determined not to freak my shit. Probably my pursuers didn't share my commitment to

making me rich. They'd let me go for almost four years because . . . some scary spy plan? I was playing Mad Libs with a
story I didn't know. But if it wasn't about making me money,
then it had to be they'd forgotten about me, or, worse, they
wanted the hacked chips deployed. And if they'd wanted all
those backdoors installed, it was inevitable that someone eventually might like to know how they worked. That answer could
be found only in my head. I'd encrypted the code that used the
exploit. Even if I'd missed a node in my cleanup, and I thought
I had not, they'd need my passphrase to see how it all worked.
Maybe if they'd captured enough transactions over time, someone smarter than I was could have reconstructed it. Maybe the
guys in the lab, if they still worked there, could access the chip
without my coaching, but today's pursuit suggested I possessed
something my watchers did not.

I stared at the dingy blinds and watched the lights come on
outside. The plaza rumbled with the diesel growl of trucks
idling, pulling in, pulling out, drivers eating slick hot dogs off
the roller grill, waiting out their mandatory rest periods before
moving on with pallets of important stuff. These were people
with places to be. I'd been sixteen when Mom died. Every night
since, I'd taken a moment to appreciate that no person anywhere could possibly be thinking about me. A girl could do a
lot with that understanding. Ten years later, I knew that invis-
ibility had failed: someone had come looking and I'd missed it.
It's a hazard, I suppose, of being someone that hasn't mattered;
I'd covered my eyes and believed myself unseen.

I sat for a long time. I'd loved my little underground money farm with its steady secret harvest. Maybe that attachment had left me flat-footed when it was time to leave. Now I considered the likelihood that my activities hadn't been secret. Why would these guys be pursuing me, unless they were hoping to use my chips for their own purposes?

I'm a patriot, of course, but not a patriot who trusted the stooges chasing me, whether they worked for the United States or for the Death Star. I had no impulse to donate my work to their cause. It was one thing to levy a citizen's tax on some un-evolved banking institutions; it was a whole different thing to imagine a predatory governmental entity that could walk through all those doors to do whatever they chose. This was my pizza-box-in-the-paper-recycling error. Without intending any specific harm, I'd engineered access to a large number of networks. It was access that couldn't be revoked without throwing a lot of equipment worldwide into the trash, what we'd call a forklift upgrade. I hadn't considered that anyone else would learn about my chip or want to use it for more than a little gentle pickpocketing. I couldn't let those men find me.

I was starting to be afraid. If a charging bear wants your sandwich, you drop the sandwich. But what if that bear wants your brains? Speculating about the particulars of my impending doom was hungry work. I imagined a wild mushroom bourguignon, with extra sour cream, on homemade egg noodles; also garlic bread, very buttery, with broiled mozzarella and parmesan on top. I stood up. A voice in my head said, "Hide,

hide, hide!" But I knew I needed to move. It was time to visit the diner, and find a way out of California. The laminated card by the bed advertised Comfort Food. Comfort sounded good. Comfort sounded better than wild mushroom bourguignon.

20

RUTH

DINNER IN THE DINER

The 49er Diner was more what I expected than what they advertised. The Uber Eats signage seemed a little ambitious, unless the drivers were ordering delivery to the parking lot. But it was clean enough in poor light, and the food smelled OK. I checked out the pie case and looked around. There were trinkets, prepacked cinnamon rolls of the heavy white frosting subtype, packets of Tylenol and Tums, road maps.

"Do not steal anything," I reminded myself. Nothing that fit in my bag would help me here. There was a TV on local news and two waitresses. The older woman was serving the back section, so I went to the hostess stand and asked for a table in the far corner. I studied the menu. Here's a social puzzle: What does a youngish woman alone order in a truck stop diner to signal to an older woman that she's trustworthy, not a junkie, and needs help? I decided the answer wasn't salad. Or tri-tip. I settled on meatloaf, even though I hate meatloaf and was starting to feel like any meal might be my last at liberty. Imagine if they locked me up, and I spent my natural life remembering my last meal at liberty as truck stop meatloaf?

Plenty of people eat solo in those diners, many of them regulars. Under the shifting layer of families and transient travelers, there's a community of sorts. It's a place you can be as well known as you want to be. I picked resolutely at my meatloaf when it came, thought about my problems, and waited for an invitation.

Her name tag said Louise. She stopped by with the coffeepot and a ceramic mug. "You want coffee, hon? A piece of pie?"

I let the "hon" touch me. I pushed back tears (remember that I was tired, scared, and eating meatloaf). "Coffee, please," I said. "Black. But I'd better skip the pie." Sugar is the wrong choice when you want to prove you're not a junkie.

Louise poured me a cup of coffee. Set it next to my plate. She eyed the loaf wreckage. "It's not that good today. You want me to bring you something else?"

I smiled. "No, thank you. It was fine. I'm not as hungry as I thought."

"You want a box?"

"No," I told her, "I feel bad wasting food, but I can't take it with me."

She cleared the plate without comment, and I sat for another half hour or so, nursing that cup of coffee. I was waiting for her to come back, and she did. She freshened the cup, stood for a moment, and asked, "Everything all right, then?"

I let her see my face. "Not really," I said. "I need a ride." I watched her register that, then added, "I'm running from someone. I had to leave my car. I have some cash, so I can pay my way, but I need to get out of here." She waited in silence. I added, "He's a cop."

She studied me carefully, not unkindly. "Roll up your sleeves," she said, and I did, turning my arms so she could scan my veins. "And if I checked your legs and feet?"

I shook my head. "I'm clean. You're welcome to look. I have big problems right now, but it's not drugs, and I swear I'm a safe passenger." I met her gaze. "This is hard, but I really, really need help. Do you know a driver that might let me buy a seat out of here? Anywhere works."

She looked around the room. I saw her consider it.

"Maybe," she said. "There might be someone." She turned back to me. "You got a name, hon?"

"I'm scared to give it to you," I told her. "Call me what you want."

Louise chuckled. "You look like a Mary," she decided. "I'll call you that." She scanned the diner again. "The man I'm thinking of hasn't come to dinner yet, but I saw his truck pull in. You can wait here, if you like. I'll ask him for you when I see him." She smiled a little. "I know what trouble is; I can see you're in it. He's a safe ride, Big John. He's odd enough; they all are here, but he won't hurt you."

I thanked her. I felt a moment of hope. I wrapped my hands around my coffee cup and settled in my chair to wait.

21

MIKE

SEND IN THE CLOWNS

There were too many people in the room by an order of magnitude. I grant it had become necessary to brief my superiors. At the least, I needed personnel and vehicles to intercept Ruth at the border, and we would need to expand my program when she gave us access to her chip infrastructure. Nevertheless, there are times when the definition of "need to know" becomes critically important. Many people drive cars; it's a relative few who need to know exactly how they operate. Likewise it seemed obvious that most of my colleagues did not need to know about Ruth, her compromise of worldwide networks, or the specifics of the previous twenty-four hours. I crossed my arms and caught my boss's eye.

"Sir."

"Mike? What? We're still waiting on a couple folks here." He carried an impressive stack of paper for not knowing anything.

"Sir, I wonder if we could speak privately first."

My boss, Gary, looked at Earl, who sat next to me, studying his phone. "It seems to me," Gary said, "that this extracurricular caper of yours has been a bit too private for a bit too long." Earl coughed obnoxiously.

I clenched and released my toes in my shoes. Seven times, then I could speak calmly. "Sir, I understand that this all seems somewhat chaotic. But there are aspects of my operation that remain extremely sensitive. I will need additional resources to locate my . . ." What was the word for Ruth, in this context? I was not Dr. Frankenstein, so she was not technically my creature, not exactly. For one thing, she was lovely. For another, she could hide. "My asset. But what she has done, the reason we need to find her, that's something that should remain closely held." He looked unconvinced. "Sir, it's a matter of national security. The potential threat is significant."

Gary sighed. "Earl?" Why was he asking the know-nothing consultant who lost the car?

Earl set down his phone. "All I can say for sure is that she smoked us twice in one day. Mike hasn't shared all the interesting details." He looked deferentially at Gary. "I'm as eager to hear it as you are, sir."

I pushed out of my chair, turned my back on Earl. "In the SCIF, sir, if you would." And I walked out of the crowded room toward the secure briefing facility. Gary followed—and Earl.

I had to tell them most of the story—her hands-off recruitment, my choice to follow her on her microchip investigation, twisting arms to get myself that channel sales job, then the carefully planned customer call that dropped her just down the hall from our Red Team lab, camouflaged as a commercial test lab. I described what she had done with that discovery, as far as I understood it. I might have served myself better leaving out the first years of Ruth's supervision and development, but I wanted to emphasize our unique connection, and I dislike lying. Also I was delivering up to my country an extensible, operational, and tested exploit infrastructure; that should have balanced out some minor missteps.

I finished my brief, and there was a moment of silent immobility. Gary and Earl were staring at each other. Then Gary slammed his hands onto the table. "This is fan-fucking-tastic, Mike. We knew you were using all that equipment to snoop on some girl, but holy prophet on toast, I had no idea how far out of bounds you really were." He shook his head, took a breath, turned to me. "And this Ruth, with the keys to everything, she's where now, exactly?"

I held his gaze. He owed me a round of applause and a promotion, at least, but I could wait. "She's driving to the border at Oroville, sir. In that Corolla."

"You know that?"

"I know her, sir."

He snorted. "Earl?"

Earl said, "I don't think we know where she is. Canada doesn't make sense to me."

"Any guesses?"

Earl scrubbed at the grain in the table. "I think she'll have ditched that car. She has to know we've identified it. It may still be at the Walmart. I feel like she'll be trying to drop out of sight. That's easier for her in the US."

I wrapped both hands into fists and tucked them under the table. Here was the guy who saw one preview, lecturing us on the movie.

Gary sighed. "I don't need to explain what it means if someone else picks her up first, Mike. Any sign at all of someone else watching or helping her?"

I shook my head. "No."

"Earl?"

Earl shook his head. "No, sir, and her chips are online in some interesting places. There's just that goofy engineer she took to the Caymans, and it's not clear what he knows." I must have shown surprise—Earl had been deep in my business without my knowledge or consent.

Gary smirked. "Mike, did you think you were invisible? Earl's been looking over your shoulder for a while now. I told him to give you a long leash." He frowned. "Probably a mistake."

"Sir." I controlled my tone. Time was the priority, and Ruth. There was still a way for this to work out properly. "Sir, I can see I should have told you all of this sooner." I swallowed. "Much sooner. But Ruth, this asset, she is playing for our team. We just scared her today." I glared at Earl. If I'd gone in alone like I'd wanted, no guns or foot soldiers, the afternoon would have ended differently. "Let me go to Oroville. Let me talk to her. She'll make the right choice."

Gary and Earl looked at each other again. Earl shrugged. "It's a long shot."

Gary sighed. "OK, Mike. You can take a chopper up to Oroville to see if she shows. Earl goes with you. I want you in constant contact. And straight back here if we find that car or she doesn't show." He loosened his tie. "I'll check with the crypto team on that menu. Maybe they've found something. And let's send some guys to collect her accomplices. Should be easy enough to spot two fools dragging a multimillion-dollar mattress through Sunnyvale. We should be able to get that done, at least." He thought for a moment. "I want them off the street. We may need them for leverage."

I said, "Sir . . ."

He said, "I appreciate you've tried to keep this quiet. That was not a strong play. If we don't collect her at Oroville by tomorrow at twelve hundred hours, I want her face everywhere: local news, everywhere." He checked his watch. "Make that twelve hundred hours today."

Earl looked up. "What'll we say she's done, sir?"

Gary stood. "Double murder. Her friend Thom and the other guy. That should shake her loose. Come on."

For the first time, I saw Ruth might end up in real danger. I needed to get to Oroville, to intercept her, and persuade her to join me on our mission.

Gary had his hand on the door. "We need to get the team up to speed, searching for her. You have some good current pictures, I'm assuming?"

22

RUTH

HITCHING A RIDE TOWARD JUDAH

Big John, when he arrived, was authentically big. He was tall and broad, with the slack power of a man who'd done hard manual work for years before quitting it for a sedentary life on the road. He'd been large long enough to own shirts that fit; he was bald and wore a Yankees cap. He was also odd, as promised. He carried a God's Gift paperback New Testament in his shirt pocket (even with readers, the type was too fine for him, but he claimed to have it memorized). He ate more bananas than seemed possible. You know how there are bananas at every truck stop checkout register? Big John was why. Also he wore a Ruger SR1911 Commander nominally concealed in a shoulder holster (anything a man that size can reach will print against his clothing when he sits, and the holster must have chafed because he adjusted it constantly and unconsciously). My Guns for Dummies class was finally proving its value. It helped a little to know I could at least point and fire what he carried, even if his vast size meant I'd have no chance to take it from him. Big John's name, when I finally snuck a look at his driver's license, was Ezekiel Archibald Arnold.

I sat and watched him eat three full plates of the meatloaf with mashed potatoes and extra gravy. When he was done, waiting for dessert, he put down his napkin and spoke to me. "I don't care much about your story. Louise says you're running from a cop husband, and I can see for myself you don't chatter. I'm a man of good works. I also could use the cash." He wiped his mouth carefully on the back of his hand.

I waited.

"I'll take you to Cheyenne for three hundred, if you can follow my rules." I nodded. He went on. "Money up front. My cab, my way: no drugs or other bullshit. No smoking, and that includes those fucking vape pens." He looked at me and continued. "I pray often. You can join me or not, but you'll respect our Lord in my truck. No cursing."

I nodded once more.

"I won't harm you in any way. But you may see some things. This isn't a normal commercial run. We'll be taking an alternate route. When we get to Cheyenne, you'll forget me, and I'll forget you. Is that clear?"

"Yes. That works for me," I said. "I'm not in a hurry to get anywhere. And I'm grateful." I meant it. For the first time all day, I could see myself getting away.

Big John waved his big hand to dismiss my thanks. "Louise says you're a fellow traveler. We're meant to help each other, when we can." He caught the waitress's eye. "Hey, darling! Another piece of pie here for my ride-along." And we each had a decent piece of coconut cream pie with toasted almonds and vanilla ice cream before we rolled out of the 49er Travel Plaza, headed east on Interstate 80.

23

MIKE

RUTH MISSES
HER MARK

We rode together to meet the helicopter. We sat in the back of the Agency sedan like small children compelled to church. I had an irrational urge to kick the seat in front of me. Earl turned sideways. He held out his hand. "Hey, Mike, I'm sorry to have blindsided you. Gary insisted I keep a low profile, but you must be feeling pretty shit about all this." Management consulting forms probably required apology training. They should have, anyhow. I ignored him, and he took his hand away. We rode for a while, through the early hours of the city. Then he said, "Can I ask you something personal?"

"Sure."

"Did you have money growing up?"

It was a strange question. "No. I mean, not really. We were middle class."

"You go to private school? Summer camp? Your folks own a house?"

"Of course, yes. But I don't see what that has to do with anything."

Earl laughed softly. "I thought so. No, man, I'm not insulting you. It's just, that's something you maybe don't get about Ruth. She really seems to come from nothing, you know? She's poor. She's not going to flee to another country like a rich person. She's going to disappear like a poor one. This Oroville trip is a waste of time." He read my silence, and added, "I researched her, obviously, once I knew she mattered."

Ruth's background was irrelevant, like studying an eggshell to predict the flight path of a dragon. But it bothered me that Earl might have some facts I had not troubled to collect. "She's not poor now. She's stolen at least fifty million dollars." I fought the anger in my voice.

"Doesn't matter," said Earl, smugly. "She only knows one way to run."

"So don't come with me, if you're sure she won't be there."

"Oh no," said Earl, stretching his fingers. "Your job is to find Ruth. Mine is to follow you. It's your monkey and your circus. I get paid no matter what."

We didn't speak again until we'd waited for hours at the border in Oroville, until it was clear that Earl had somehow guessed Ruth right, and I, uncharacteristically, had called her completely wrong. All he said then was "Come on. We'd better get back before Gary writes a headline and releases the bounty hunters. You're going to want to rein him in, if you can." I swear he sounded sorry for me.

24

RUTH

WHY DOES EVERYONE HAVE TO BE CRAZY

Big John drove an older Freightliner Cascadia raised-roof tractor with a seventy-inch sleeper. It was gray, dusty with some dents, unremarkable. It seemed small with him in it. Cleaning was not his thing. There were layers of trash on the floorboards: food wrappers, empty cups, an abused paperback copy of *Codependent No More*. There were other things too, harder to identify, and I briefly wondered if he traveled with a cat.

"I don't care when you rest," he told me, "but I sleep in back overnight from eight to five in the morning. You'll stay up front. You can have the sleeper during the day if you want it." I didn't want it. My optimism had left me; I was twitchy and haunted. The sleeper seemed like an extra-stinky cell. I wouldn't even see them coming. I stayed up in the cab, waiting out the night with the seat reclined, watching out the window for a creep in a suit.

Our route was indeed alternate. At Auburn, we took the exit and drove to Grass Valley. There, Big John met a man by the side of the road, and they loaded four large burlap bags into the trailer. We continued to Loyalton for another meetup, then backtracked to Portola, and on up to Janesville. In each place, we found a pickup waiting, mud-slathered plates, and the driver with Big John would carry a few more bags of something to the back. Before he got out of the truck, Big John would pause, bow his head, close his eyes, and pray. He did it again when he got back in. Each time he said something different and stopped to listen for an answer. His voice rose and fell, pleading sometimes, or bemused, but mostly patient, soft, adoring. I could not have joined in if I'd wanted to. Prayer was not a ritual for him. It was an immediate personal conversation. Big John prayed with more attention than he drove.

We stopped to eat in Susanville. I stood outside the truck and stretched in the sunshine while Big John went inside for sandwiches. He took it for granted that I should stay out of sight, which made life simpler. He came out of the store, tossed me a bottle of water, then held out two subs for me to choose between. They were both labeled Italian DEE-LUX, so I took the nearest. We leaned against the warm grille. Big John said grace, and I waited for him to finish before eating. He unwrapped his sub, took a huge bite, chewed ten times, swallowed, and asked me, "OK then?"

I knew what he meant. I'd been watching for half a day while he collected bags of something in sketchy back-road meetings. This was my moment to ask a question. I picked a raw onion out of my sandwich. And another. The sandwich was full of stupid onions. I peeled back the top of the roll. I was going to smell them all day, but I didn't have to taste them. "Yeah, OK," I said. "I told you, I'm not in a rush to get anywhere." I'd decided I didn't care what was in the truck, that I felt safer riding with a man who had his own bad thing to hide. He was bound to be more careful. He would avoid attention. I liked it.

Big John held out his hand. "I'll eat those, if you don't want them." Which I didn't like as much, but I gave him my wad of raw onions. Then we got back in the truck and headed off to more meetings. I didn't care, but still I kept count. By the end of the day, we'd collected forty-four bags of something. OK, not just something. One guy hadn't remembered to put his delivery in burlap, so by late afternoon, I knew for sure we'd collected forty-four separate fifty-pound bags of ammonium nitrate fertilizer. The bags looked sealed, but I knew Big John's trailer wasn't air-conditioned. I started to care a little. One long day's work, and we were hauling more ammonium nitrate than McVeigh had used for the Oklahoma City truck bomb. So that gave me something new to think about.

25

MIKE

RUTH TAKES A RICOCHET

When I predicted that Ruth would drive north, I underestimated the external influences on her flight trajectory, and the power of her unschooled instinct. Without my benevolent containment, she took her cues from coincidence and feral impulse. The rational choice would have been to rendezvous with me. Instead, she ricocheted. It was only when Gary called to say that they'd found her Corolla (and our SUV) that I accepted she'd probably never tried to reach Oroville. Something or someone had interfered with her. It was time to act humble. I couldn't risk reassignment.

I decided to start with Earl. "So, you called that one right.

Where do you think she is? What's your gut?" We were heading back into the conference room. I was braced for a reaming.

Earl made what had to be his thinking face. I wondered if he practiced it in the mirror. "I'm not sure exactly. I feel like she'll have left the area. We can be reasonably certain it wasn't on a plane, a train, or a bus. We're watching those. But I don't know." He grimaced. "It's easier to guess what she won't do than what she will, don't you think? She'll need help. Does she have any family or friends you know of, beyond the clowns we have already?"

Me, I thought. *I'm all she's got.* I shook my head. "I've never seen anyone."

He rubbed his forehead. Sighed. "Well, she has cash and a pretty face. She's making her way somehow. Shall we go try to stop Gary from driving her into the sea?"

To his credit, Earl tried. He and I agreed, for once, that a public nationwide manhunt would not call her to us. But Gary didn't buy it, and Gary was in charge. He imagined that any person helping her would immediately desist, place a call to our anonymous tip line, hold her until we got there, and collect our reward. Gary couldn't imagine that someone might prefer assisting Ruth to collecting a bag of government money. He didn't consider she had money of her own. He had no concept what he was chasing.

I convinced him, at least, to use one of Ruth's photos in the blond wig, even though I knew she'd ditch it immediately. That photo was a private message, from me to her. Who else could have it? It reminded her I was still here, protecting her as well as I could, and also that I was waiting.

RUTH

FRAMED BY
MURDEROUS CREEPS

We spent the night pulled in behind a farmhouse in Lakeview, Oregon. I lay back in the passenger seat, listening to Big John snore in the sleeper. I tried to remember what little I'd ever understood about ammonium nitrate. It needed heat to detonate, I thought. Was that all? I was a thief, not a terrorist. I had no idea. I hadn't expected that question on the test. For the millionth time, I wished for my iPhone and Google. I also wanted to check my email. Thom and Toby should have sent something by now, to let me know they were OK. I sat sleepless. Being rich was kind of a bust so far. Toward dawn, three bighorn sheep tiptoed in front of the truck, silhouetted against the mountains in the silver early light. I watched them and imagined us all blowing suddenly to bits: me, Big John, and three luckless sheep.

We made fewer stops our second morning, and we picked up different things: two large spools of wire and a stack of crates that might have been turnips or baby blankets but probably held something sinister. Big John was cheerful. He detoured for special waffles and brought me a plate to eat in the truck. We stopped for showers at a small plaza with no visible cameras. It was a good morning. I let my mind slide ahead to Cheyenne and what I might do after I kept my bargain to walk away and forget Big John.

Those thoughts occupied me until midafternoon, when we pulled back into the Flying J at Grass Valley, and Big John's phone rang. He checked the number and answered.

"Yah, darling? What?" Long pause. He glanced at me. "Well, shoot now. Yes, I will. OK, thanks." He hung up. "Stay in the truck," he told me, and climbed out of the cab. He left her idling at the pump and walked inside. After a couple minutes he came out carrying a *Mercury News*. His face was flushed clear to his ball cap. He flopped the paper into my lap. Not waiting to fuel up, he pulled out of the plaza toward the interstate. They had my face, a little blurry, wearing my blond wig. The headline read **Crazed Local Coder Girl Slaughters Friends and Flees in Apparent Heist Gone Wrong**. *The Merc* never expected anyone to read past the bold print. They had company headshots of Thom and Toby, and a crappy crime-scene view of their bodies splayed across a mattress in the street. The public was warned not to approach me. I was armed, dangerous, unstable.

"I'm going to puke," I warned Big John, and he pulled a KFC bucket from the floor and handed it to me. He gave me a couple minutes. Then a couple more.

"So that's you in the photo?" he asked, at last.

I nodded.

"You kill those boys?"

I shook my head. "No. They're friends of mine. Well, one is. Was? I didn't kill them. I didn't know they were dead. They were fine yesterday." My face felt weird, and I touched my cheek: tears.

John merged onto the highway. I thought about Thom and Toby, rushing home to claim their money mattress. What had happened? I'd halfway expected them to get caught, but killed? It made no sense. And I had no idea why my picture was there, in that wig of all things. I couldn't understand it. If a random villain shot them for the money, why would my wigged self be implicated? If our pursuers had found them, why were they dead?

Big John spoke again. "So, is it a cop chasing you?"

"Not exactly. I said that because it sounds less crazy. He works for, well, I don't know what agency."

"The government?"

"Yeah."

"The United States government?"

"Yeah." I'd decided that had to be true.

"And this guy, he's your husband?"

"No. Louise guessed that, and I didn't correct her." I thought for a moment. "It's more than one person. They want something I built. And I don't want to give it to them. Really they have it already, but they can't figure out how to use it."

"So they're chasing you, and you're telling me they also killed your friends? And made it look like you did it?"

I knew how mad it sounded. I couldn't help it. "Yes, they're chasing me. And maybe they killed my friends, but I don't know. And someone put the whole thing in the newspaper. But I can't say why. I don't understand that at all. I can't believe any of this is happening." I had air but felt like I did not. I told myself I was as safe as I had been before I saw that paper. But that wasn't true. My team was mostly dead now, and Big John was deciding again. I had no plan if he chose to kick me out of the truck. Even if he agreed to finish our trip, what then?

Big John flipped his indicator, merged into the right lane, took the exit. He turned onto the frontage road and stopped on the shoulder. He turned to face me. His color was normal again. He said, probably louder than he intended, "They're chasing you, but are they tracking you? Have they been watching us all along?"

"No."

"No? You say that, but can you prove it?"

"Sure I can. So can you. If they could find me, I'd be dead or locked in a box, not on the front page of some random newspaper in a blond wig." I looked at him. "Think about it. We wouldn't be sitting here if they knew where I was." I folded my hands. I sat as still as I knew how. "I swear to you, Big John, I didn't hurt anyone. I may be a sinner, but murder's not my sin."

Big John looked at his hands, then back at me. He adjusted his holster. "I need to pray." I sat back and closed my eyes to wait. I'd have prayed too if I'd thought it could make a difference.

We stayed awhile. Finally, John seemed to reach a conclusion. He sat up behind the wheel. He cleared his throat. "Mary," he said, "I believe God intended that we should meet."

I could not think of one safe reply. I waited.

"Do you know what the Second Amendment is?"

I nodded, trying to guess where he was headed. We had God and guns in the cab now, big bomb in the back.

Big John rambled on. "But do you know what it means? Why it's there?" He didn't wait for a response. "The Second Amendment is not about owning novelty weapons. It does not exist so some asshole can shoot a moose with a full auto or take down his shitty neighbor. The Second Amendment empowers us to raise arms against our own government. Our forefathers knew. They knew that power corrupts, that we citizens would need to fight back." He leaned his face down into mine. He really did smell like onions. "You've seen what I'm doing?"

"Sort of. You're not collecting Toys for Tots. I know that much."

He laughed. "No. That's right. I am not. You and I, Mary, we're soldiers in the same great army. We're fighting back against a government that has turned on its own people."

I kept quiet. Big John sounded like he'd still take me to Cheyenne. He also sounded insane. I wished Louise had found me a different odd ride. I started planning my first big meal when I got away from him. I knew it was a fantasy—the food is terrible in Cheyenne, and my face was everywhere. Even so, I imagined spring rolls stuffed with fresh herbs and shrimp, a hot broth with lemongrass and noodles, followed by coconut red curry with crisp vegetables and chicken, all over jasmine rice. Then I felt bad. My friends were dead and I was hungry. I deserved whatever came to me.

Big John put the truck back into gear. "Don't worry," he told me. "I see that I'm called to bring you with me. God's will be done. It shall be revealed as the need arises."

"Thank you," I whispered. I flipped the paper so I didn't have to see my own face or my friends' bodies. I looked out the window and tried to pretend I was getting away. I guess I was still crying.

27

MIKE
1-800-STUPIDS

Halfway through that endless second day, Earl passed me a note. It read *World's Shortest Drinking Game: 1) Post reward for pretty girl; 2) Drink on every tip.* He wasn't funny, but he also wasn't wrong. Gary's campaign to expose Ruth had buried us instead, like Wile E. Coyote under a landslide of ACME Great Ideas. I could almost hear Ruth calling "Meep, meep!" as she roadrunnered out of sight. I took comfort that any real sighting would be utterly obscured by the thousands of fake ones. I wanted her found, just not by the brutes Gary had recruited to follow up any tip deemed to be credible. Fortunately, he had no method to make that determination.

Where was Ruth? We had too many answers now. Was she buying bronzer in Santa Barbara? Riding a red road bike south toward Big Sur? Had she taken an Uber to Hubbard County, claiming claustrophobia? Had she picked at midnight meatloaf in Sacramento? The sightings rolled in. We took reports on neighbors harboring aliens (space type, mostly), domestic violence, and three different locations for Jimmy Hoffa's body. We answered our phones, entered pointless reports into a wildly bloating spreadsheet, and rolled our eyes at each other across the table. Except Gary, who was performing essential interagency liaison tasks, probably playing solitaire in his office.

Around 1400 hours, I capped my pen and logged out of my extension. I retrieved my dopp kit from my desk drawer. Since I'd realized I might imminently be in person with Ruth, I had taken more care with my grooming. She deserved that consideration. I could provide the elegant frame to her beauty in our partnership, just as my discipline would add focus to her raw energy. I realize that structured facial hair can be a fatuous choice for some men. Mine was sophisticated without ostentation. Women admire the look, though some pretend they do not. I was anxious for Ruth to see me up close. I inspected myself in the mirror and snipped a few rambunctious hairs. Our relationship was about to change, and my hair was ready. Soon, I promised myself, it would be Ruth watching me. I could sleep, while she wondered what I was thinking.

I put the kit away and walked downstairs to sit outside. The sparrows were fighting over crumbs in the grass patch by the front entry. There was a single wet brown sock stuck to the sidewalk. Somewhere, a car alarm sounded. I sat on a damp bench. A woman can be right there, and then she can be gone. Nothing

I knew about Ruth gave me the smallest clue where to find her. I had imagined she would find me, reach backward through the lens, take my hand, and join me on this mission, whatever it was.

I have always been a patriot. But I did wonder, sitting there, if there might be some authority other than my boss that might be better trusted with Ruth's hack, once we got it. Gary was acting like a thug. Small wonder she was hiding. It would take an exceptional stroke of luck to find her now.

28

I MAYBE SHOULD HAVE ASKED WHAT "ODD ENOUGH" MEANT

From Grass Valley, we headed to the Pilot Travel Plaza in Fernley, leaving the highway and winding carefully along back roads to avoid the scales. We weren't heavy, but Big John was leery of the cameras and load declarations. I should have felt protected, but I'd decided that he and I might not play for the same team. Which in hindsight seems obvious. He was the enemy of my enemy, but riches and bombs have a troubled alliance, historically speaking. His "God and Guns" speech had rattled me. More important, Big John's behavior changed after he saw that newspaper. It wouldn't mean anything to say he was acting strangely, but his weird took a new form. He got nosy.

Maybe an hour after his "soldiers in the same great army" declaration, as we rolled through Emigrant Gap southwest of Truckee, John reached across and shut off the radio. He'd kept it set continually to indistinguishable (for me) evangelical AM stations, and I would have said I'd tuned it out entirely, except for the great silence that fell when finally it stopped. He glanced at me. "So what's your plan when we get to Cheyenne?"

"My plan is to forget you, like we said."

His big fingers drummed on the steering wheel. "Do you have people there to help you?"

I can't say why I resisted that question. I know I started to fidget. At last, I said, "You know I'm so grateful for the ride. For everything. But you've done enough. I don't see how we can help each other at the end of this. You said we should forget each other, and you were right."

"I said that before I knew you."

"We still don't know each other. Not really." I made myself sit still. I sat on my hands. I forced myself to pay attention, to concentrate on disarming his pride and whatever urge to control drove his questions. I had nothing waiting in Cheyenne, but suddenly I was anxious to get there. "My only friends are dead, and I don't know why. Probably it's my fault. And you're tougher than they were in a million ways, but you don't need the hassle, right? You don't need more eyes on you."

"I can look after myself."

"And after me too, I see that. But I have my own code, you

know? And I won't dump my trouble on you." I didn't add, my code is also not to blow shit up. But I thought it so loud, he may have heard it anyway. I could tell my nonanswer pissed him off. It ended the discussion, though. I was fine with that.

"OK," he said. "It's your call. I was just trying to help." And he turned the radio back on.

How do I feel when a man says my life is my call? Not grateful. I started to wonder what to do about the cargo in that trailer. To interfere is never my preference. I won't tell a strange woman to sober up or to stop hitting her kid; I drive my car on Bike to Work Day. Watching Big John assemble his DIY Big Bomb was starting to feel like my business, though. And he was pissing me off.

Apart from one stop for restrooms and a bag of sunflower seeds (Big John was hooked on the dill-pickle-flavored Spitz brand), we drove straight on. Just shy of Fernley, he left the highway and wound his way to an old boarded-up barn with peeling paint. Behind it sat another dented gray Cascadia with a raised roof and large sleeper. As we pulled up next to the other truck, I saw its plates were a clone of ours. "This will only take a sec," said Big John, and he climbed down and walked to the other truck. He retrieved a folder of paperwork and a small black box. I watched the other driver get out with a pair of license plates and walk back to swap them onto his truck. Big John opened his driver's door and peered into the space above the pedals. "Can you help me?" he asked. "I can't figure out where this goes."

"What is it?"

"It's the commercial GPS tracker. My buddy brought it direct from Sacramento on I-80." He grinned at me. "And he got all the scales paperwork. He drove his truck with a copy of my plates. He's our alibi. Can you help me install this?"

I stayed put. My nope alarm had gone off. "You're not the guy who took it out?"

"Well, yeah, I am. But I can't see how to put it back."

I leaned over. There was a neon-green round 9-pin connector near the floor on the left-hand side by the driver's door. "Maybe try that green plug," I said, and sat back up.

He looked. "Right. I knew it came from down there somewhere." He plugged in his box. "Thanks." He sounded aggravated. Did he think scut work would convert me? I wasn't his gofer.

The doppelgänger truck honked and pulled out. Big John waved, pulled his seat belt across, and followed it to the highway. We turned east again at I-80 and finished the drive up to Fernley.

29

MIKE

HIGHWAYS LIKE GAME TRAILS

Earl came out the front entrance, looked around, then joined me on the bench. Have I mentioned he was a leg jiggler? Earl was one of those guys who seemed judgmental of stillness. Even when he sat, he moved. So he came to sit with me, all the while radiating the energy of a guy who wished he were somewhere else, and then another place after that. We had that in common, at least. I also wished him somewhere else.

"Something's come up," he told me, then lapsed into vibrating nonspeech. It's not a proper silence with that much air displacement. He considered me. "I want to tell you, and I don't. Because I can't figure you out, Mike. You did ninety percent of this amazing thing. But now it's like you're maybe sabotaging the last ten percent. I can't tell why."

I watched his foot. I wondered if everyone had the urge to clobber Earl. It might not fix him, but it couldn't make him worse. On the other hand, he'd been an ally trying to contain Gary. And he could make a troublesome adversary. "Bringing her in isn't the last ten percent," I told him. "It's a hundred percent of what's next. That's what I'm realizing. You call it the last ten percent and you start to hurry, get sloppy. I got in a hurry too, so I'm not criticizing. I'm talking about my own mistake right now. I'm just saying that bringing her in isn't the last little bit left to do. It's a whole new thing, and it's not inevitable. I fucked up before because I didn't understand that." *And neither did you*, I thought, *or Gary*, but I didn't say it. Ruth was mine, after all. I should have kept her in line.

He thought about that. I waited. Finally he said, "There's a woman I worked with running domestic ops over at Homeland Security. LuAnn. Smart lady. Tough. She grew up doing guided hunts in the Teton backcountry." I clenched my jaw and braced myself for a stupid fucking story. Maybe, just maybe, there'd be a fortune in this cookie. Probably not. Probably it would end with Earl telling me to be the eagle, and I would have to hit him after all.

He continued. "She and her family took rich people on trophy hunts in Bridger-Teton. You know, some wealthy guy with time off, a hundred grand, and a space on his wall for an eight-by-eight monarch elk. The clients would fly in for a week or two with their private planes. She had to meet them and drive them around. Keep their boots clean, and their glasses full of single malt and all that. And then of course get them onto a horse and up the mountain and find them a trophy bull to shoot, then all down the mountain and home in one piece. I guess she got tired of that. Anyhow, she has a theory I like. She says when you're hunting, you find the right game trail and let the target come to you. And she also says, when you're hunting people who aren't rich, the roads are the game trails. Rich people have boats and planes, but the rest of us end up on a highway." He kept talking, and Ruth was getting further away. I couldn't see her. I was getting used to that feeling. Earl went on. "She's put together an undercover network of long-haul truckers to track and sometimes intercept bad shit with domestic terrorism." I looked up. He nodded. "Yep. One of them seems to have acquired a passenger."

I jumped to my feet. "They're sure it's her?"

"Pretty sure. And the timeline works. He picked her up at the Sacramento truck stop two nights ago."

"Eating meatloaf?"

"What?"

"Never mind. One of those stupid tips. Where are they? Is she safe?"

"Safe enough, I hope. LuAnn says her guy is for sure a bit of a sicko."

"Oh, brilliant. And where are they?"

Earl stuffed his hands in his pockets. Pulled them back out.

"Well, that's the catch. The driver is undercover, and close to a big bust."

"Drugs?"

"No. Explosives. He's hooked into a domestic terrorism cell. He got tapped to transport a load of ammonium nitrate for some kind of attack. LuAnn wouldn't say where they are."

"What?"

"Yeah."

"Ruth is riding with an undercover domestic terrorist sicko on a pile of volatile explosive material heading to an attack, and your friend says she's safe?"

Earl made a face. "I mentioned something to that effect. LuAnn may have said that she's safer than our front-page dead witnesses. At any rate, it's a big operation, and LuAnn says she won't fuck it up to assist the recovery of a single unrelated asset."

I forced myself to stand still. "Hell."

"Yeah. I wasn't comfortable disclosing Ruth's actual value."

I hadn't thought of that. One leak the wrong way, and the domestic evil actors might have their hands on a bigger weapon than any amount of fertilizer. The word "safe" seemed less and less applicable. Ruth had chosen a terrible escape route. "That seems like the right call. Who else have you told?"

"No one yet. I just now talked to her. I came to find you first." He looked at me. "We're on the same side, Mike. By me, this is still your operation. I thought we might brief Gary together." He held out his hand, and this time I shook it.

30

RUTH

OLD-DOG DREAMS

At the Fernley Pilot, Big John parked at the far end of the lot. It would be the darkest spot and the most private. If the trailer suddenly exploded, we'd kill fewer people. It was also the longest walk to the restrooms, past the most lookers-on. I knew there was no good choice. I knew my creeping mistrust had to be pathology—fear, grief, helplessness. I felt like my brain had been hit with a sledge. I needed to think, make a plan, figure out what was happening. I couldn't even choose a soda. It didn't help that Big John was hovering. I'd come out of the restroom, and there he'd be, checking the posters pinned to the wall. I'd step out of the cab to stretch my legs and so would he. I ended the day crouched in the cab of the truck, arms around my knees, just waiting for him to go to sleep so I could freak out in peace.

At eight p.m., bedtime for Big John, he tapped me on the arm. "How's about you take the sleeper tonight," he offered. "No chance you're seen back there."

I held my face blank. Why was I suddenly so suspicious of him? I was sure if I went into the sleeper, he'd shut me in. "That's nice of you," I said. "No. I'm better up here where I can see."

He frowned. "It's no good for either of us if someone recognizes you. That's just common sense."

"I know," I said, "and I'm sorry. I just can't. I promise to keep out of sight. But I can't be in the sleeper." And I waited. Would he grab me? I had no chance against him, and we both knew I wouldn't scream or struggle.

I watched John consider it. He flexed his hands, shifted his weight back and forth. I expected him to start praying, but he just sat there for a while looking at me. Then he sighed. "You're making a mistake. It's a stupid risk for you to stay up front, but I won't force you." He looked around the plaza. "We can't drive on tonight. I'm pushing my hours of service as it is. We have to wait at least ten hours to move."

"I understand."

"I'm on your side," he told me. "I should think you'd know that."

"I do," I said. "I believe you." But I didn't. So I sat frozen in the cab, hair drawn across my face, and waited for him to go to bed. Then I waited for his snores to announce he was no longer watching me. It took a long time for him to sound like he was asleep.

I was tired, and I knew it might be a while before I could make myself rest. Every light inside my head was stuck on. It felt like I'd forgotten how to sleep and might never remember. So I sat. I let myself think about Thom. I remembered our trip to the Caymans to open the shared account. We'd spent an afternoon shopping for trinkets for Toby. We'd eaten shaved ice at every meal. We'd taken a sunset catamaran. I rarely do fun things. That trip had been part of my plan, but it had also been a good time. I wondered again who had killed them.

Then I thought about that newspaper photo of me. It was blurry, like a still from a video. It had been taken up close, from a low angle. I'd been turning my head, so the camera had been on my right side, a little behind me. Like it was in the car on the drive to Sacramento, the only time I'd worn that wig. There must have been a camera in that shoulder bag. Thom had wanted it gone, and I'd humored him. He'd been right. And that photo had to come from the people who'd been watching me. Surely they knew I'd left the wig in the Walmart bathroom. Why not a different photo with my normal hair? The only possible explanation was that they wanted me scared. Well, they were doing an A-plus job of that. Killing my friends had probably been enough; the wig photo was just showing off. So my pursuers were sadists. My eyes drifted around the darkening cab. Maybe it was a flash of passing headlights or maybe I was finally looking. I saw it at last, anyhow, centered under the dash. About the size of a drugstore gumdrop, it was a lens, tiny shreds of plastic where it had been installed quickly or carelessly. I'd run out of the lion's claws, straight down a snake: there was a camera in Big John's cab.

It must have been there all along. I realized that much. He'd had no chance to install it since Sacramento. Maybe his boss made him drive with it? An insurance thing? I didn't believe that. He knew that camera was there, and he hadn't warned me. It was pointless to disable it at this point. It would just tell him I knew. I felt a click in my head, and I made a decision. It was time to take a chance. I slid my hand into my bag, nested in the trash at my feet. I pushed aside the cash and pulled out one of my burner phones. As quietly as I could, alert to any change in John's noises, I lifted the door handle, cracked the door, and slid out of the truck.

It was a mild night, and I felt better in the air. Of course I couldn't run, not here or now, with my face everywhere and no plan. But outdoors, not running felt like a choice. I walked in the dark, away from the cab, toward the fringe of grass at the edge of the lot. A ways down, an old trucker stood with his older dog next to the trash can. They looked at me without interest and stumped off together, stiff legged. *If I survive this*, I thought, *I'm getting an old dog*. I wondered what old dogs liked to eat. Probably soft cat poop, but I imagined baking cookies shaped like dog bones. His muzzle would be sugared with age; he'd have crazy old-dog eyebrows. Maybe he'd sleep with his head on my foot while I sat reading literary fiction. I shook my head. First, I needed to survive.

I'd pitched the card but learned the number. I took a breath, let it out, then dialed. He answered right away. "Hello?"

I didn't hang up. I steadied the phone. "Gideon?"

The silence seemed long. I opened my mouth to tell him who I was and why I had his number. Then he said, "Ruth?"

"Yes," I said. "It's me. You told me to call."

"Hang on," he said. Then, "I stepped out of the lab. I'm still at work, but you probably guessed that." I hadn't. He and his coworkers seemed part of the past, but of course they still existed and were hard at work trying to break into my chip. He said, "I've been hoping you would call. Are you OK?"

I stood in the lot, watching Big John's truck for any movement. "I don't know," I said. "I thought I was safe, but I'm not. The guys chasing me, I think they're your guys; they killed my friends and set me up for it. I hitched a ride and now the driver might be out to get me." I was babbling.

"That's a lot," he said carefully.

"I sound paranoid. I hear that. But I just found a camera by my seat, and he's hauling more than two tons of ammonium nitrate."

I heard him exhale, a low whistle. Then, of all things, he chuckled. "You're kind of a freak magnet, Ruth." I could hear him thinking about what I'd told him. It was oddly comforting. Anything could have happened to me at that moment—he was far away—but I felt less alone. Then he said, "I'm sure you've thought about this. The camera and the explosives don't usually go together."

"That's why I'm calling you. You're part of the whole government spook situation, right? Can you look this guy up in your spook database for me?"

"Maybe," he answered, and I could tell he didn't like being called a spook. "Probably. But I'm going to have to sneak around . . . spookishly. It might take me a day."

"I'm sorry," I said. "I'm a freak magnet because I'm a bitch, I think."

"Tell me his name, Ruth." I told him.

"My turn," he said. "I don't suppose you'd like to give me a hint? You do good work, by the way. I'm proud of you. Except you're now a wanted criminal."

"I can't," I said. "If I tell you how it works, they can kill me too. I'm alive because they need my brains inside my skull."

"Are you serious about that?"

"You don't read news?"

"I do. Usually. But this week I'm living in the lab because some insane genius freak magnet woman built a secret backdoor in a chip and then installed a hundred thousand of them out in the world."

"Two thousand."

"I think my number is better than yours, in this instance," he said.

My stomach clenched. Why so many? How had I missed that? "Shit," I said. "That's a lot." I hesitated, then went on. "So, I made the mistake of bringing on a guy to help with scripting. He and his boyfriend just got killed in Sunnyvale, and someone is framing me for it. They're using a photo of me from surveillance footage. It's front page of *The Mercury News*."

"Damn," he said.

"Yeah."

"You should have learned how to script."

"I get that."

"I mean, you can hack a microchip, and you won't bother with a little coding? What's the matter with you?"

"I get it!" I said. "And I'm sorry. I'd take it back, but they're dead." I was crying now, quietly.

Gideon sighed. "OK. Let me find out what I can about this guy you're with. Can you call me tomorrow?"

"Yes. Unless we blow ourselves up."

"Yeah. Well, no scuffing your feet. Extinguish all smoking materials." I could feel him smiling down the phone. "Ruth?"

"Yeah?"

"The menu. Want to tell me anything about that?"

"The what? What menu?"

"They found a menu in your apartment, hidden in your violin case. Some items were marked. The prices are prime."

"Oh God." I almost laughed. "I like nice food, Gideon. Those are things I hoped to eat someday. When I was rich and safe. It doesn't mean anything. I thought I'd thrown it away."

"Ah. Well, that's a hundred man-hours wasted. And another thousand saved, I guess, so thank you."

"I owe you."

"Call me at lunchtime tomorrow. Be careful until then. Maybe we'll share that nice meal when this thing is over."

"Thanks, Gideon." I'm sure he heard it in my voice. This would never be over. "Good night." I ended the call. It was past midnight. I listened to the low rumble of the semis. I stomped the burner on the asphalt and threw the pieces in the trash. Then I walked back to the truck.

I climbed in quietly. The snoring had stopped. Big John was awake.

"I'm sorry," I lied. "I needed the restroom." He was sitting up in the sleeper. I had no idea whether he'd seen me on the phone. "And I called my mom. She's scared to death."

"Oh," he said. Then, "I'm not your jailer. I got worried when you weren't here."

"I'm OK," I told him. "No one saw me." I waited a moment. "Thank you."

I curled back up in the seat and pretended to sleep. Once Big John was snoring again, I jammed my bag up against the camera. Then I closed my eyes and waited, trying not to think, for morning.

31

MIKE

IT'S HARD TO
FIND THE GLORY
IN MOST MEETINGS

In the cage match of Gary versus the rugged ex-outfitter LuAnn, it wasn't close to a contest. Even as he yelled and threatened her and stomped back and forth in front of her desk, she took off her glasses and cleaned them on her sleeve, set them down next to her phone. Covered a yawn.

"That move?" hissed Earl. "It means he's not worth the ammo." He liked her, and I might have too, except she sat between me and Ruth. Even so, it was fun to watch Gary take a thumping. Finally, she timed out. She put her glasses back on and stood up.

"I appreciate your concern," she said, "as much as I can with such minimal disclosure. You have your reasons, no doubt." She picked up a sticky note, examined it, and put it back down. This woman actually had a maroon blotter on her desk. I wondered if there was a vintage stationery closet somewhere in the building. That could explain a lot about Homeland Security, if they were running around mimeographing things, making carbon copies. She also had a high-end lightweight laptop driving three supersized retina displays and a gold-framed copy of the Lord's Prayer in crayon block letters.

"My guy," said LuAnn, "is due to arrive in Cheyenne, Wyoming, sometime in the next twenty-four hours. We have a team in place to intercept his contacts when they take possession of the explosives. My people will stage his arrest and secure your girl at the same time. That's my offer. He knows who she is and will keep her with him, unharmed, until then. If he can. She's not his top priority." She looked steadily at Gary.

This pause was his opportunity to explain the urgency. She knew our problem was bigger than some killer on the run, even with two bodies on the front page. But Gary hesitated. He studied the carpet. His left eyebrow twitched. I thought he would have briefed the operation then, if he'd understood it better and been able to explain it without asking me to step in. He shook his head. "Need to know, I'm afraid. I'd hoped you might trust our judgment on this."

She smiled unkindly. "We'll hold her in Cheyenne," she said. "Keep your phone on." She looked over his shoulder at me and Earl. "Gentlemen," she said. We were done.

Earl elbowed me as we walked back to our own conference

room. "Did you see that?" he muttered. He sounded pleased. "The women are *owning* us on this op!"

"How fun," I told him. I didn't mean it.

The room was crowded, and our briefing was long, an update on every kind of waiting. Gary seemed relieved to tell the assembled team that Ruth had been located, sort of. He'd found a large paper map of Wyoming, probably next to a stack of those antique blotters. He'd stood it on an easel in the front of the room, and he kept pointing to it. We heard from forensics and from the various surveillance crews. We heard a dozen government synonyms for "failure."

The final update was from the tech lead, a pale skinny guy who looked like he'd slept in his clothes, probably on a floor. I remembered him from the chip lab: Gideon. He'd been my contact when I sent Ruth in, so many years ago. Gary partially cleared the room, a nod to his need-to-know compliance. "To date," Gideon told us, "we've found no undocumented method to access this chip. We began with the expectation"—he corrected himself—"the hope, that she had duplicated a known prior method. That approach has not proven out." He looked like he'd rather be playing *Dungeons & Dragons* or whatever those people like to do. "We also hoped to find that the base chip was modeled on one of three prior releases from the same company. It was a solid guess and might have provided a leg up by letting us compare the hacked item to a known"—another self-important pause—"that is, a presumed-clean version. That solution also is looking unlikely, though we have not completed our review." He looked almost pleased, and I thought,

He admires her; he's enjoying this. "Our options going forward are limited to brute-force analysis, which would be quicker with additional equipment, or some kind of inside tip." He looked directly at Gary. "Without guidance from the original designer, it's going to take a lot of luck, sir, or years, potentially. That's the math." He went on. "The crypto team has also completed its analysis of the proposed cryptographic key retrieved from the apartment."

Gary moved. He had been listening. "The proposed what?"

"The menu, sir. And it's a menu."

I stood up. "It is not just a menu. It's a key."

He turned calmly to me. "It's not. Or, it's not a key relevant to our objective. It has no connection to this investigation."

"You don't know that."

He smiled a little. Smug jerk. "I do. We have mathematically eliminated it as a potential key, either for the interpretation of the chip design or as a potential access method to the passphrase for the cryptographic component of the software overlay."

"Blah, blah, blah," mumbled Earl. He was tapping the table with both index fingers.

Gideon went on. "I'm glad to review that math in more detail, if you're curious. I'll need the whiteboard, and it might take a while to walk through it."

Gary made a frustrated noise. "No, we aren't doing that. No one's questioning you." He looked at me. "Right, Mike? It's a menu. We know at this point she doesn't leave keys lying around." He turned to Gideon. "Thank you. We'll move on." Gideon sat down.

Gary reviewed, with some gloss, our agreement with Homeland Security. He made it sound like a positive interagency collaboration, but there was no missing our near-total lack of useful information: where she was, where she would be, how we'd get her back.

One of the boys still sitting in back raised his hand. "Sir? I wonder if you can comment on Homeland's operational instructions?"

Gary's eyebrow twitched again. "Instructions?"

"Specifically, sir, I'm wondering if they're authorized for lethal force, if it looks like she's going to get away from us again."

Silence. I heard myself say, under my breath, "Fuck."

Gary controlled his eyebrow. "The plan of record is retrieval. That's all we're discussing at this time." He gestured again at the map and picked up his papers. "I don't have to remind you all that if we find her before they do, we maintain control." He paused. He set down the papers. "But I can't dismiss that question entirely." His eyes flicked over to me. "If we have to choose between an unanswered question or some wild card roaming the world with the answer in her head . . ." He shrugged. "There's a decision to be made. That's all. We meet again at eighteen hundred hours. How's about somebody finds her before then."

Everyone stood to go. Gideon was still in the room. He approached Gary. "A word, sir?"

Gary turned. "Yes?"

"I'd like to request protection for the lab and its staff."

"Protection? Why?"

Something came and went on Gideon's face. "You've said your target is a double murderer, that she killed two people with minimal understanding of her technology. My lab poses a much greater threat to that chip, and she knows it."

Gary said, "Somehow I doubt she'll risk coming back to stop you guys."

"You've said she stole a lot of money. I imagine she has the resources to outsource that work."

Gary said, impatiently, "Ruth poses no continuing threat. You'll have to take my word on that."

Gideon studied him. "OK," he said. "I hope your word proves out." And he left the room.

"Tech guys," said Gary.

Earl shrugged. "It was a fair ask."

I watched the two of them, and thought about Gideon's request. I'd missed something.

32

RUTH

SAVED BY TRUCK STOP SUSHI

We left Fernley at six. I was sick from lack of sleep, laminated in road grit, guilt, and dread. I alternated between the urge to talk again to Gideon and anger that I was dangling on his input. My planning had narrowed to the single question of when to leave the truck. I couldn't begin to visualize even the first hundred yards after that.

Focused inward as I was, I didn't notice that Big John also had not risen fresh to greet the sun. Seventy-five miles west of Winnemucca, I felt the truck veer and correct. I looked up to see him soaked in sweat. His usual background mumbled prayer had somewhere mutated to a tight loop of "Oh fuck, oh fuck, oh fuck, oh fuck." Cursing in the truck. End times. A wave of lethal flatulence broke across the cab.

There's a children's book, *That's Good! That's Bad!* Maybe you know it. I'd encountered it on a thousand-time repeat, trapped next to a mother and her small son on a cross-country flight. The story presents disastrous cartoon-jungle hijinks that somehow come right, with a refrain of "Oh, that's bad. *No, that's good!*" All this to say, when Big John's GI disaster began, I didn't recognize the "that's good!" turn that it was. I simply thought we'd crash and die, onlookers unwilling even to crack a cab door as we drowned, both of us, in an ocean of toxic diarrhea. And then the truck would explode.

In hindsight, I'm convinced my reflex to trust my instinct, that nope alarm, also made me vulnerable to useless premonitions of doom. I'd drifted into the belief that Big John's unwavering ritual of prayer conferred a genuine advantage. Nerves and vestigial superstition had convinced me his fortunes trumped mine. I would gladly have challenged him to poker, but never roulette. So it shocked me as much as John when my own Lady Luck, incarnate as Our Lady of Food Poisoning, cast her nasty eye on the four packs of truck stop sushi that Big John had ingested, in and around his ominous nighttime lurking and terrorizing. During our time together, he'd proven impervious to vast consumption of convenience store delights: loaded hot dogs, gelatinous nachos, pickled things (all kinds), and floppy pizza glossy with pepperoni. The man's gut had seemed invincible. But that morning, the sushi mustered itself to strike a gruesome blow.

John swerved recklessly onto the shoulder. He threw the truck door open and shambled brokenly across the weedy grass, dropping his trousers on the way. "Don't pick roadside flowers," the wise women say. I didn't watch what happened next. I would have pitied him, if I'd feared him less. As it was, I pitied myself and began to expect a longish delay.

At noon we arrived, finally, at the Flying J in Winnemucca, bypassing the Pilot. Without comment, Big John angled into a spot adjacent to the restrooms. He hadn't spoken for hours. I think he could not. Clutching the waistband of his flannel monkey pajama bottoms, he staggered toward the showers, dragging a bag of laundry. My general aversion to the sleeper cab was now specific. One more place never to bring a black light. I guessed we were going to be parked for a while. I put on my ball cap and sunglasses, grabbed my bag, and followed John to reserve a shower.

Gideon answered on the first ring. "Ruth? Where are you?"

Paranoia clutched me. He couldn't be on my side. I was imagining this because I couldn't accept being alone. I was jumping from trap to trap.

"I'm sorry," he said. "That was a bad question. Just tell me: Are you anywhere near Cheyenne?"

"Not really."

He exhaled hard. "OK. You're still in the clear. And I have news. Are you somewhere secure?"

I'd decided to call him from my shower unit. "Yes."

"OK, Ruth, listen. That guy driving you? He's undercover for Homeland Security. There's a big bust coming in Cheyenne."

I guess I'd half expected something like this since last night. I examined the grout in the floor; it might never have been new. I wondered why a public shower would choose light grout. If I opened a truck stop, my bathroom and shower color scheme would be black mold. I took a moment to be relieved that Big John wasn't plotting to blow up a crowd of innocent puppies and babies, that I wasn't obligated to risk myself stopping him. I let myself like him again for an instant. Then I sighed. Things were getting more complicated. "Do they know I'm with him?"

"Yes, they know. They're planning to grab you somewhere during the bust. Ruth, you need to get off that truck. Do not go with him to Cheyenne. You aren't safe."

"What are you telling me?"

"I don't trust them. There are too many guns involved, too many dicks swinging." A faint chuckle. "Apart from your stellar instinct for companions, you have a gift for triggering male anger. You may have noticed."

He had no idea. Stupidly, I asked, "Are you mad at me?"

"No," he said. "No, I'm not mad. I'm trying to help, but it's hard to see a path through this thing."

We were quiet. I felt hopeless. I wondered if it was time to pull a Butch Cassidy and go out in a blaze of gunfire. I was sad that my last meal would have been a shrink-wrapped pack of serrated orange crackers with a smear of stale peanut butter.

"There's something else," Gideon said. "Your friends? There's something off there."

I guessed "off" was a new euphemism for dead. "What do you mean?"

"The whole setup felt weird. So I tried requesting protection, in case your murderous self brought down a hit on the lab. They dismissed me completely. There was awkward eye contact."

"Huh, well, I'm not likely to circle back. Especially since you have years of analysis left anyhow."

"Funny," he said. "I always thought you were a funny girl. I reminded them you're extremely rich, allegedly. You could outsource."

"Damn. That's true. They weren't worried?"

"They were not, and get this, after they said no, I went over to the morgue. I told the attendant I wanted to search your friends' effects for clues to help me break into the chip."

"And?"

"And they aren't there. No wallets or pockets, and no bodies either."

I thought about that. "So where are they?"

"I don't know, Ruth. All we have is one picture and a fake news story. I can't prove it, but I think they aren't dead. They may be chained to a wall somewhere—probably they are—but I think they aren't dead."

I felt a surge of adrenaline. He should have told me this part first. Maybe Thom and Toby had been caught because they were stupid, not killed because I was lazy. I spoke without thinking. "Fuck, I'm hungry."

Gideon laughed. "There she is! God, you sounded like a zombie. I was worried about you."

"I'm lucky to be alive. Big John ate truck stop sushi. He almost wrecked the semi."

"That may violate the terms of his undercover contract."

"If you're right about Cheyenne, that sushi may have saved my life."

"I'm right about Cheyenne." His tone changed. I heard voices in the background. Gideon said, "Dad? I'm going to have to let you go. Call me when you have results."

"Goodbye, son," I said, and listened as the line went dead.

I took a shower. I trashed my burner and took a chance (in hat and sunglasses) buying two more phones, some snacks, orange Gatorade, a bottle of water. Half the people in a truck stop look like they're traveling in disguise, but my new hope for Thom and Toby probably affected my judgment. I even stole a pocket atlas to plan my escape.

33

AENEAS DIDN'T HAVE TO DEAL WITH THIS SHIT

I put some effort into studying that stupid paper map. There was nothing else to do. With a start in Sacramento, a Class 8 truck loaded with explosives, and an end point of Cheyenne, I concluded they'd be traveling I-80 east. Not a lot of choices once they entered Wyoming; no other route made sense. They had to be getting close.

I told Earl, "If your girlfriend in Homeland Security would just collaborate, we could have resources in place."

Earl coughed. "Some people care about legal jurisdiction."

"What's that supposed to mean?"

"Come on," Earl said. "We're all being grown-ups about it,

but everyone knows this entire project was illegal. Every part of it. You aren't meant to operate domestically at all."

I caught that "you." Earl was evaluating his options.

"Define 'illegal.' I was recruiting."

"Uh-huh. Even if you can convince me that years stalking a solo hacker counts as recruitment, and she's not acting very recruited right now, the rest of your project colored way outside the lines. Homeland would be within their rights to take over the whole thing."

Since the morning meeting, I'd been churning over the lethal force question, and its unpalatable answer. Now, here came another sickening thought: the boots-and-dogs people getting their mitts on Ruth and maybe access to her hack. "I guess they'd better not find out about it. Right now they think we're just chasing a runaway criminal."

"Hopefully they think that."

"Hopefully?"

"LuAnn isn't stupid. You know I agreed that story was overkill. Between that and all the anxious senior guys begging for updates . . . Let's just hope she's too busy with her bomb plot to get curious."

Gary stuck his head through the door. He glanced around and came in, the very embodiment of an anxious senior guy.

"Sir?" I could tell he didn't bring great news.

"Just an update from Homeland." He had his morale-building voice on—it was definitely bad. "They're delayed. LuAnn's agent has a virus."

"He has a virus? He stopped for sniffles?"

Gary turned his palms up. "No details. She just said he's slipping by at least a day."

"And Ruth?" This was Earl.

"No mention. We're assuming she's still with him."

"So"—and I knew I wasn't helping—"the dog ate Homeland's undercover agent? We're actually going along with that?"

Gary's expression changed. I remembered, belatedly, that all government authority was sacred to my boss. "Mike, I must remind you that we are only *in* this situation due to your nondisclosure and mishandling of a very dangerous individual over a period of *years*." He raised his hand. "No. There will be a time in the future to defend yourself. Accounts will be balanced, mitigating factors considered. The job at hand, our sole priority, is to resolve your fiasco with as little damage to the Republic as possible." For the first time, I wondered what might happen to me personally at the close of this exercise. The awards and promotions, clearly deserved, seemed increasingly remote. Gary nodded to Earl. "I expect you two will formulate an approach for bringing this girl into compliance, once we have her in custody." And he walked out of the room.

Earl looked after him, his expression unreadable. "Shit, dude," he said, finally. "You could have handled that better." I noticed he'd stopped calling me "boss."

34

RUTH

OH GOODIE, LARAMIE

Big John was propped by the passenger window, watching Netflix on an older Dell laptop. He moved back to the sleeper when I tapped on the door. I climbed in, suppressing any thought of seat cooties, and handed him the Gatorade. Knowing his affiliation had settled my nerves. We were allies again, except the part where he delivered me to my death at the hands of a mob of murdering government dick-wavers. I guessed he didn't control those decisions. I noticed he'd draped a sweatshirt over the dash. We were off camera.

"You OK?"

He gestured shapelessly. "Not quite as dead as I have been. Thanks for this." He indicated the drink. "We've made shit progress so far today." I didn't grin, but considered it. He picked at the Gatorade label. "I think I'm OK now to drive."

"We're going to Cheyenne tonight?" I hoped my stress sounded like excitement.

He seemed not to register it. "We need to get close, if we can. Maybe Laramie. I'd like daylight for the actual delivery." His tone was so neutral, I had a moment of doubt. But he'd been bullshitting scarier people than me for a long time. I reminded myself, he must be good at his job. I was not his priority, just a bonus or an added complication, depending on how his compensation was structured.

"Um, all right. Can I do anything to help?" Laramie might be survivable, I thought. It had vaguely urban bits. I could probably hide, for a while, at least.

He shook his head. Gathered himself, and crawled into the driver's seat. He mumbled a prayer, put the truck in gear, and we left Winnemucca.

35

THE OPPOSITE
OF BRIEFING MAY
BE LONGING

A big hint dropped when Gary and Earl left together for Cheyenne. Gary made a point of delegating the San Francisco operation to me. "So there can be no question about your role," he said. They were cutting me out. I would be far from the action, the credit, or the chance to help Ruth. They'd waited for the evening briefing, moved up an hour to accommodate their departure. I assumed the public spanking was to ensure that my colleagues, now nominally my direct reports, knew better than to support any private initiative. Gary and Earl didn't stay for the rest of the meeting. There had been no progress tracking Ruth or accessing her chip; they expected any breakthrough to come in Cheyenne. Behind Gary's back, Earl raised his phone, pointed to the screen, and mouthed—well, I don't know what he mouthed. I'm not a mind reader, as recent events had shown. I assumed he was either promising or requesting a back channel. Possibly both. I'd observed that Earl's late-breaking involvement in my operation was working well to his own advantage. His impact on Ruth's fate, and mine, had been more difficult to evaluate. I couldn't guess the details, but I sensed he and Gary were heading toward an unpleasant surprise in Cheyenne.

The men filed out, chatting among themselves, planning where to meet later for beer. Not knowing Ruth, they had no sense of imminent loss. For my part, I decided to try once more. I took out my phone and composed a text to Earl. "I am aware that my judgment has been inconsistent. Please consider the likelihood that Ruth will have identified that truck's cargo, even if she has not discovered the affiliation of its driver. She will not risk being present at a terrorist rendezvous. It is a certainty she will leave that truck before Cheyenne, probably wherever they stop when the driver's hours of service are up." I paused to proof my message. I considered adding contractions to sound more relatable.

"Are you sure you want to send that?" I looked up to see Gideon reading over my shoulder. "It won't make her safer." I gave him a stern look, but he ignored it and went on. "If they catch her now, they'll bring her back in pieces."

"What are you suggesting?"

He shrugged. "Paint the door and watch her find it. Isn't

that what you told me years ago, when you wanted her to see the lab?" Those had been my words, back when I was in charge, when things were going well. I'd forgotten that. Gideon smiled. "Good advice then. Better advice now." And he walked out of the room. I deleted my draft text. Of course it was good advice—I'd said it first, and I'd created her. Who better to escort her in? I repeated my own words to myself like a mantra. It was nearly 2400 hours when I stood up from my desk and realized I had no idea what they meant.

36

RUTH

ROACHES IN THE SHADOW OF A GOVERNMENT SHOE

Big John could not sit up, yet he drove on, hands clenched on the wheel. I watched him from the corner of my eye. He looked genuinely ill. His prayer had lost its sweet conversational vibe. It had become a desperate pleading loop, just below the edge of hearing. Sweat beaded along his forehead and soaked the back of his shirt. He'd forgotten his bananas. This wasn't all food poisoning, I realized. It was terror.

I thought about Gideon counseling me to bail. I didn't want to ride into a confrontation between bomb-building nutters and macho armed law enforcers, especially if the well-funded team carried bingo cards with my photo in every square. I'd be alone with no weapon or vehicle, and my prize, if I escaped, was Cheyenne. Not tempting. But the I-80 corridor through Wyoming was a lousy place to jump off: long stretches of lonely road with a scattering of desperate urban settlements, all stuck to the highway like gravel on dropped gum. Hitchhiking was illegal. How long would I, with my Most Wanted features, last out here? Gideon hadn't thought it through, I decided. He was a lab rat and hadn't studied this section of interstate. Still, part of me had to wonder if maybe he had. He'd helped me so far. He'd saved my ass. But why? He wanted something. They all did.

I mistrusted Gideon's advice, but I was also tired of huddling in Big John's cab like a witless loser. The people chasing me seemed mostly stupid. They expected me to run, fuck up, get caught, and confess. Or bleed out. It was time to teach them something, and chance had offered me an excellent instructional tool. I looked at Big John and made my decision. I was going to steal his truck. I couldn't hope to overpower him or to drive a semi loaded with explosives; I would have to steal the driver as well.

A sign made it thirty miles to Elko. I reached across and switched off the radio. The camera was still covered. I turned in my seat. I reminded myself that John had taken me on with no notion of my history, that he had his own skin in the game, that he looked like a man who might want a new choice.

"The people you work for, do you trust them?"

Big John glanced at me, then back at the road. His hands shifted on the wheel. Eventually he answered. "I put my trust in God. He shows me where I need to go. My employers are just part of His Plan."

"What about me? Am I part of His Plan?"

"Everyone is. Even if they can't see it."

I took a careful breath. "John, I think we might be afraid of the same people. I can get us out. I mean, we could do it together, but I would need your help."

This idea made contact. He looked at me, and his foot lightened; the truck slowed ever so slightly. Then he sighed. "You have no idea how powerful they are, Mary. They can see our every move."

"There's another tracker on the truck?"

He nodded. "Under my seat."

"Pull over and show me." He shook his head. "Seriously, John. Why do you think the government guys are chasing me? Show me the tracker. What harm can it do? If you don't like my ideas, you can always hit me over the head and throw me in back with the bomb powder."

"I'm already late. They're waiting for me."

"Exactly."

He glanced over.

"They're waiting. Let them wait. What are they going to do if you stop awhile for fuel? They know you've been sick, right? They know what you're hauling. I'm guessing they don't want to improvise. They're going to wait."

He was considering it. "Do you have people, John?" I asked him. "Is there somewhere you could hide, start over?" His eyes, I saw, filled with tears. He didn't answer. It wasn't a no.

For days I'd tried to look harmless. Now I wondered how a super-capable person who also was not a double murderer would look; I tried to do that. "I need to pray," he said. And he did.

Big John took the exit at Elko and pulled in at the Sinclair. He parked on the dark end of the lot. He shut off the truck, pocketed the keys. He gestured me over to the driver's-side door, pulled down a magnetic panel above the steps, shone his flashlight onto the battery array. There it was, wired to the nearest unit. A light blinked as it updated his overlords. "Don't touch it," he warned me.

I put my hands in my pockets. "Can you take a picture of the cover for me? I want to see the serial number." He pulled out his phone and took a picture.

"If you disable that thing, they'll know."

"I get it," I said. I studied him cautiously. What made a man end up here? Were they bribing him? Blackmailing him? I formulated my approach. "Look, John, I'm a hacker. I broke into a bunch of government stuff. They can't figure out how I did it, so they're after me." I couldn't see his face clearly; the man loomed over me in the darkness. "I think I can fix this tracker situation, but you would have to tell me who put it here. The tracker isn't the problem; it's the system watching it. You would have to trust me."

Big John stood for a long moment. Then he put his hand on my shoulder, hard. He pushed me down onto the asphalt. "Kneel," he said, and I knelt. I mean, I had no choice. Big John dropped awkwardly to his knees next to me. I bowed my head.

I was scared again. He started to pray. "God, guide me in this. Have you sent an angel to deliver me or a devil to test my faith?" He peered at me dubiously, and I tried to look angelic. "Give me a sign." We waited. And waited. I heard traffic passing on the road. There was a high whine from the lights. Big John emitted a residual intestinal grumble and shifted uncomfortably. He decided, "God wants me to follow my gut." I bit my lip. No laughing. He looked at me. "What's your real name, Mary?"

"Ruth."

Big John sighed. "Ruth the wanderer. Ruth the lost. Ruth the faithful."

Silently I added, *Ruth the desperate.*

He struggled to his feet. Offered me his huge hand. "Get up, Ruth. God wants me to trust you. Show me your plan."

I stood and brushed the dirt off my knees. "I'm going to need to use your laptop."

I worked slowly. This was not a time for careless errors. First, I removed the keystroke logger and disabled the software monitor. Big John watched as I configured VPN software, enabled encryption, and generated keys, connecting through remote servers back to one of my old staging machines. In fact, I didn't know whether I could access the Homeland Security network. But Gideon had said my chip was everywhere. I wondered why he knew that. He understood what I'd built and was serious about learning how to use it. If he wasn't a bank robber, what might he be? Methodically I ran traces, attempted access. After about an hour, with Big John starting to twitch, I got lucky. I found my chip in the Homeland network perimeter. I did a silent happy dance. Hello, beloved creation! Then I generated my access sequence, and I was through. It was embarrassingly easy after that. I logged into their surveillance server through an open operating system bug and accessed the tracking database. I searched the serial number and showed John. "Here you are. This is your unit. This is how they're tracking you."

He looked at the display, impressed. "So now you delete it?"

"I don't think so." I'd been mulling over this choice since he let me stand up. "If I delete it, they rush here, to our last known location, and start searching for us. We won't get far. It's no better than smashing the tracker."

"We can't escape?"

"I'm going the other way with it," I told him. "I'm going to clone you." He looked puzzled. He actually glanced around the cab. I pointed at the screen. "See all these other entries? It's everyone else they're monitoring in this region. I'm going to modify the database so they all look like you. Then I'm going to force the records onto their backup. Then I'm going to corrupt and crash the system. By the time it's back online, it's going to look like there are hundreds of us everywhere."

"Like roaches."

"Exactly. Like roaches. It'll take them a while to stomp them all. Somewhere in there, we can disconnect your unit. But I need about an hour to set it all up." I went on. "You must have a phone. It needs to be powered off. It's better for your alibi if it's smashed and in the garbage here, but I understand if you don't want to do that."

Big John shrugged. "I'll get rid of it." He stretched. His expression changed. "You're going to need snacks. I've noticed you're better when you eat something."

He reached for the door, and I stopped him. I handed him cash. "Buy fuel too. No credit cards from now on. And no sushi, please. Just shrink-wrapped stuff."

"No sushi," he said, "and no cards." Then he grinned at me. "You're not an angel. But if you're a devil, you're a small one."

"Fighting bigger ones?"

His smile dropped. "Fighting Satan," he said. "And there's more than one of him."

37

AND GUESS WHAT—
THEY LOST HER

Just after 0100 hours, I was dozing at my desk. Going home felt like abandoning her. My cell lit up. Earl and Gary, texting and calling all at once. I answered the call. It was Earl. "Are you at the office?"

"Howdy," I said. "How's Cheyenne?"

"We have a problem," he told me, and I thought, *Imagine that.* "Homeland lost their tracking server. It's back up now, but the data is corrupted somehow."

"So they've lost surveillance of the bomb truck?"

"Maybe? Probably. I'm having trouble getting a straight answer. Oh, hang on," said Earl, "Gary wants a word."

I waited. Gary's voice came on the line. "Mike? I assume you're still at the office."

No, I thought, *I'm home with my hot wife, watching my two small boys as they sleep.* I pretended for a moment that I had everything I deserved in life, everything I'd set aside to curate Ruth for my ungrateful country. My sense of duty reasserted itself. "Of course," I answered. "What do you need?"

"I need you over at Homeland Ops. I need a status *ASAP*. Your girl has done something to the system." I heard Earl say something in the background. "No, no. There's no such thing as coincidence. Didn't you say she was a hacker?" Gary was impatient.

I said, "Sir . . ."

"Just get over there. I've told them to let you in. Call me when you've assessed the situation."

"Yes, sir," I said, and I went.

The Ops Center was chaos. I thought of their bust: just a team of domestic terrorists about to take delivery of a large bomb kit, suddenly unsupervised. I examined the wall display. Hundreds of identical nodes crawled across the Mountain West. More blinked without moving—even surveillance targets slept at night. I saw Gideon in the corner, typing rapidly on a console. That guy was everywhere. He looked worse than before. "Hey," I greeted him. "What's happening?"

He frowned. "Oh. Mike. Hello."

I gestured at the wall. "What's going on?"

He hesitated. Then, "The tracking system crashed. They restored it from backup, but the database seems corrupted. Every node looks like their guy. It's all noise."

"But one of those is them, right? And they're still heading to the meet?"

Gideon shrugged. "Maybe."

"Maybe?"

"Maybe. Maybe this is a horrible coincidence, and everything is actually on track. Or maybe their target terrorist cell has some insane talent." He looked at his console screen. "Or option C."

"What's option C?"

Gideon shrugged. Clearly not a night person. "Option C is Ruth."

"Ruth? How can it be Ruth? That's a hell of a leap. She doesn't know her ride is undercover. And even if she figured that out, how'd she get in?"

Gideon sounded impatient. "How does she do anything?" The guy was worked up.

I wanted to shake him. "She's not magic. She can access her chip, but those boards are not approved for Agency procurement. I made sure of it. She can't penetrate the firewall." He looked at the big monitor in silence, then back at me. "No," I said. "You can't prove it. You're blaming her for a Homeland screwup."

"You're right," he said. "I can't prove it. Someone has erased the proof. And Homeland has definitely screwed up." He went back to his console. I saw he was searching through log entries, attempting a postmortem on the server crash. It looked like gibberish. If she'd done it, she'd have wiped the record. I knew that much. He was wasting his time.

I stepped away to call Gary. "Sir? Yes. I have an update. It's not great news, sir." *Take a number*, I wanted to tell him. Welcome to my world, looking for Ruth.

38

RUTH

BIG JOHN'S
BRILLIANT PLAN

Big John revealed a surprising aptitude for fuckery. Ten minutes out of Elko, he unplugged the cab GPS unit, clipped the wires on the camera, disconnected the tracker, took a small back road, and tossed all of it with his phone into the vast manure lagoon behind a dairy. He gave me a look and I didn't ask. If his last three passengers were lying like unlucky dumplings at the bottom of that, did I want to hear the story? I did not.

We left the interstate at Wells, heading north on 93. The radar showed heavy cloud cover in southern Idaho, and John claimed to be worried about helicopters. "They'll sit tight in

Cheyenne until they're certain we aren't coming," he told me. He was feeling better, eating his third banana. "I'm guessing that's noon tomorrow, unless something changes. Eventually they'll dispatch choppers from Cheyenne backtracking along 80 to Elko, looking for the rig. They'll be expecting a breakdown, maybe even a wreck, since I won't have called to check in."

"Wouldn't a wreck leave a hole the size of a city block?"

"Yeah, it could. They'll be thinking about that too." He tossed his peel out the window. I imagined robot tracker dogs scraping it up, snuffling his DNA, their artificial eyeballs glowing red. "When they don't find us, that's when they'll need to pick a story."

"As in, did you run or get grabbed?"

"They won't think I ran." He was sure. "And they know I'm not smart enough to ditch the tracker. They'll think someone took me. They just need to decide who that was."

"What are the options?"

"Well, those men waiting on my delivery—if they caught a whiff of Feds in Cheyenne, they might have intercepted me."

"Could they have taken out the Homeland server?"

"No. And I've said as much in my reports. They're aggressive enough to kidnap me, but they don't trust technology. And they suck at it." He looked at me. "The guys chasing you. Do they know what you can do?"

"Some of them, yeah."

"So maybe you kidnapped me." He laughed aloud. "Or maybe my bomb boys found us both, coerced you into hacking the server, and me into driving." He pondered this option. "In which case, we'd be fucked. They'd find bits of us in bird shit across six states."

I wasted several minutes trying to name those states. It was two in the morning. We had a few hours before daylight, when we needed to be out of sight. I felt nauseous. The rig seemed huge and obvious. Big John reached over awkwardly and patted my hand. "Don't worry," he said. "God will protect us. And I have people with a ranch outside Jerome. That's where we're headed. We can hide there."

So the turn north was not about cloud cover. Big John was driving casually, one hand on the wheel and the other resting on the door handle. His left foot tapped along with the overnight praise medleys on the local Christian AM station. How often had he fantasized escape, waiting and hoping for the tool to come to hand. I'd been that tool, arriving at the last possible minute to pluck him off his masters' map. His interminable prayers were answered, and the route lay clear before him. We were living Big John's plan, not mine. As if I'd had a plan. I wondered where he was taking me, and whether I would be a guest, a hostage, or a prisoner.

What would Gideon say about my situation, if I asked him? For a moment, the urge to find out was so strong, I considered crawling into the sleeper and calling him on the burner. But the sleeper was still and forever a Toxic Waste Exclusion Zone. And how exactly could I justify that call? To hear his voice? To have someone enact concern for my fate? It was consoling to talk to him. I wondered if his agenda, whatever it was, could execute compatibly with mine, whatever it was. But I could not visualize a world where my secret was shared and I was safe. Gideon's recent advice had been weak, at best; at worst, it had been sabotage. I needed to resist my impulse toward companionship. Loneliness was not terminal, I reminded myself, unless I let it get me killed. I stared out the window for a while, and then I fell asleep.

Big John woke me around four thirty. He'd pulled off the road into a small rest area. A sign announced a picnic table. We were, it turned out, twenty minutes from his honeycomb hideout.

"So what's the plan?" I asked him.

"That's what I want to get straight," he said. "You'll need to follow my lead. I know these people." He waited, so I nodded. "I'm going with the original story, where you caught a ride with me running from your husband. It's simpler to leave the other stuff out." He paused. "It'll be safer if you keep a low profile."

He knew what we were walking into, and I did not. "I'm not arguing with you," I said. "Your place, your rules. But it'd help to know why."

Big John rubbed his knuckles on his thighs. We were both ready to be out of that truck. "I can't explain it," he said, "but I feel like your skills might cause problems." A long pause. "Someone might take it as an opportunity. I don't want anything bad to happen to you."

"I don't want anything bad to happen to me either." I thought about Thom and his urge to turn me in. It seriously did not work out to help people. At least Big John was warning me. "So if I'm a helpless runaway, how did we get you out?"

"I'll tell them you knew how to mess up the tracker so it misreported my position."

"I can't even imagine how that could be done. It's a GPS unit talking to three satellites."

"They won't know that," said Big John. "I'm sure of it."

"OK, I guess," I said. I hate telling unnecessary lies, especially of the water-flows-uphill variety. It's just begging to get caught. "I won't stay long. I'll leave as soon as I can. I might need help figuring that out." He didn't answer. I went on. "I have to ask, because we're heading to a place that you've lived before, right? Is there anything anywhere that connects you to these people? My agency and yours are going to come looking. They're going to empty the laundry basket, go through every pocket."

Big John shook his head. "I've thought about that. No."

"You're sure?"

"Completely."

"How long since you've seen them?"

"Fifteen years. Almost sixteen," he said. "Do you have a phone? My people aren't good to sneak up on." I reached in my bag and gave him my last burner. He took it and climbed out of the cab to make his call. I watched the brief negotiation through the windshield; it didn't seem long enough to plan my murder. He climbed back in. Tried to give me back the phone, but I waved him off. I didn't share his confidence that he'd dropped out of sight.

"We're good," he told me. "They're expecting us now." He put the truck in gear and got ready to pull out. "And, Ruth?"

"Yeah?"

"Where we're going, it won't be enough to bow your head when we pray. You're going to have to move your lips too."

I nodded. Because of course. My fabulous new lifestyle continued to amaze.

A man swung a flashlight at the turnoff, then hopped onto the steps and rode down with us on a long dirt entrance. Along the way, two more men stepped out into the headlights, both wearing night-vision goggles and carrying long guns. Probably they'd been out rescuing lost fawns in the cornfield or something. Big John stopped and jumped out. He greeted each of them, formally and then with a hug. They were tall men with a common carriage, a humility that assumes immediate reward. I wondered if we were on the Arnold family compound. If so, the choppers were days out at best.

We came to a cluster of ranch buildings. The doors were open on a large Quonset. I could see a combine and a spray rig that had been moved to make room for us. Big John eased the truck all the way in. We were hidden. He cut the engine. Took a deep breath. "We're safe. Don't worry. Just let me do the explaining. The Lord has said be not afraid."

"OK," I said, then added, "I trust you," because I didn't. I picked up my bag and followed Big John.

39

A DAZZLING ARRAY
OF MORE BAD NEWS

One challenge with unauthorized domestic operations is a lack of ready resources when they go sideways. As the night wore on, Homeland insisted that everyone in Cheyenne stay in place. They were so certain their agent was on his way, so concerned about spooking their targets, that they refused to consider any preemptive search for the delayed rig. Earl told me they couldn't even leave the van to piss.

I texted him the phone number for every local car rental. He informed me that a westbound vehicle could not positively identify an eastbound truck on I-80. He claimed there was a median, no visibility, lots of gray Freightliners (he'd weaseled that much from the strike team). "Wyoming is big," he said, showing again why he made the big bucks. In the time they wasted that night, they could have driven to the last known location and most of the way back. We would have known eight hours sooner that Ruth and her sicko driver were gone.

I went looking for Gideon and did not find him. The boys in the lab were sulky and monosyllabic. They had racks of boards and servers running analysis on Ruth's chip. When I asked how long to break into it, they eyed each other and shrugged.

"A hundred years?" the hairier one guessed.

"It's not deterministic," the other one told me. "If it's a sequence, we might die of old age before we guess it. And Gideon says it's probably a sequence. We need a lot more computing power if you want this solved."

I went back to my office, but could find nothing useful to do about Ruth. I have never tried to understand quantum physics, but in that moment she was like that hypothetical cat in a box: dead and alive, on her way to me and vanished in flight, all at once.

I decided to follow up on a point of concern from my visit to the Ops Center. I opened the acquisitions database for the federal government's domestic networks and began going through the purchase requisitions. I wasn't sure, initially, what I was looking for. But just like Justice Stewart's Casablanca Test to identify pornography, I knew it instantly when I saw it. Every board with Ruth's chip had been on an Agency-wide blacklist. I had put it there as a matter of basic security hygiene. I knew the technology was compromised. It should not be installed on our own networks anywhere for any reason. Looking through equipment purchases for the last five years, I saw immediately that some-one had removed my prohibition. Over and again, her boards had been evaluated, purchased, and installed. They were in our perimeter, on the server farms, all over the black networks. There were hundreds of them. I paged through the database to see who had signed off on the recommendations. That information had been redacted.

"We're fucked." I said it aloud. "If she won't help us. Or if she decides to work with someone else. We are completely and totally fucked." I got up and headed back to the lab. I really needed to talk to Gideon.

40

RUTH

GLEANING IN THE FIELDS OF BOAZ

They had brought me to an upstairs dormitory. From the doorway, they'd pointed me toward a narrow bed by the window. It was still warm from whoever had been shifted to make a place. The pillowcase smelled faintly of WD-40. I lay down in my clothes and shut my eyes. I didn't think they would stab me in my sleep. Maybe I didn't care. I slept for an hour until the women around me started to get up for the day.

I looked around and wasn't sure where I'd found myself. I saw a large square room crowded with wood-framed single beds. It was bright with sunshine and clean. No chains clanked, no flogged children wept silently into threadbare pillows. The women were young and seemed to be behaving normally enough, apart from a shared affinity for off-trend clothing. I haven't spent time with groups of women, so I was guessing. A few groaned and hugged their pillows while their too-cheery companions tried to interest them in the fact of a new day. I was tired, I was hungry, I felt more trapped than I had the day before. I decided I played for team morning-haters.

They saw I was awake. One of them approached me. She wore basic Walmart denim, cheap socks, a blue shirt. Really it was my recent travel disguise, with the addition of a headscarf. They all wore them.

"You're up. Are you well? You came in so late. They told us not to bother you." She studied me. "Do you want a shower before breakfast? I'm Hannah."

"Ruth," I whispered. I did want a shower and definitely breakfast; I assumed Idaho should be a good bet for staples—I was in spud country now. But I decided I was best served, for the moment, by an affect of harmless traumatized weirdness. So I shuffled as far away on the bed as I could manage, wrapped my arms around my knees, and stared at her.

Her face changed. "You poor thing. You'll be safe here, you know? Everyone will be talking about what you did, bringing Ezekiel back to us." She held out her hand. "Come on. Let me show you where to wash up. You'll feel so much better." I relented and followed her to the bathrooms. She didn't comment when I carried my bag into the shower with me. I would not be separated from it. I've learned from heist shows that heroes who get careless with their cash invariably lose it. All I had was money and a secret. I was hanging on to both.

She waited for me, and when I was dressed, she made an apologetic grimace.

"Would you mind a headscarf, do you think? Of course you don't have to. But it's our way here. It might be easier." I didn't answer, so she led me back into the bedroom and pulled open a drawer. So many headscarves, clean and folded, blue mostly, a few white, one pink, a plaid, some florals, and toward the back, a single black one. I pointed to it. "Of course," she said, though I had no idea why. "May I put it on you?" I bent my head so she could cover it.

We walked together into breakfast. There was plenty of it, served family style on big tables. I saw scrambled eggs, biscuits, pork all ways: sausage, bacon, ham, boiled and fried. There was a bowl of bananas on each table. Probably twenty-five people were already seated, eating or stirring instant coffee. They noticed me with interest, but there was no sinister silence. I didn't see Big John. Hannah served me, then sat next to me. She clasped her hands and said grace, one I'd heard in the truck. I moved my lips. Years before, in a school choir, I'd sung with a gaggle of sopranos who did not learn lyrics. "We repeat the word 'watermelon,'" one told me. "It looks like words and sounds just as good." So now I bowed my head. Silently I mouthed watermelon, watermelon, watermelon. I thought, *I need to get out of here; I need to survive this*. Hannah was watching me. "OK?" she asked. I nodded and we ate. Someone had one hell of a light hand with the biscuits. Whenever I left, I was eating breakfast first.

Big John came in with two of the men from last night. He'd

washed and shaved. I saw him see me, and he raised his hand in greeting but didn't come over. Men and women ate separately, yet there was no sense of anyone enforcing rules. Hannah and I cleared our plates, rinsed them, loaded them into a large stainless commercial dishwasher. An older woman came into the room, and Hannah excused herself. I could see she was getting instructions for me.

"I'm repairing heads on one of the irrigation pivots this morning," she told me. "I'd bring you, but Deb says you're to stay. The men are meeting and asked you be here." I managed to look stricken. "Oh no," she said. She threw her arms around my neck. In my ear she murmured, "Don't be scared. We honor you. Your people are where our people come from, you know, in Bible times?" She pulled back, smiled, straightened my headscarf. "I'll see you at dinner."

The men were indeed meeting in a large room off the kitchen. Big John sat in the front. His eyebrows sent me a great big **STAY QUIET** as I walked in and sat in the corner. I hadn't planned to sing an aria. The biggest man in the room and the one in charge was Peter. I thought how the Bible namers have such a hero bias: always Jacob, never Esau; maybe an Abel, but rarely a Cain. And of course, Ruth but not Orpah, though Orpah's only crime was a home and a mother she loved.

These were practical people. Their first priority was to deal with the bomb. A guy named Nathan made that call. "We can just spray it on the barley," he decided. "Season's early enough. The plants could use the nitrogen. We'll transfer it in the Quonset and mix it like normal over at the spray station. You guys can decide about the bags. They can go in the dumpster unless you think they can be traced." He looked at Big John. Big John shrugged.

What anger was in the room, I decided, was directed toward him, not me. I was incidental. Big John was in some kind of trouble. I wondered again how he'd ended up as an undercover agent for Homeland, ingratiating himself with terrorists, fifteen years exiled from his weird wholesome homestead of Bible names and good biscuits.

"OK, well," said Nathan irritably. "Let's assume they might be traceable, then. Better safe than sorry."

"I'll bury them in the landfill," offered a lanky guy toward the back. Big John threw him a grateful look. "I'll collect them in the evening and do it after dark."

"OK," said Peter. "Problem solved. Now let's talk about the truck. That's obviously got to go. I assume it's not safe to move?" He ignored Big John. For the first time, his eyes found me. So at least one person hadn't entirely bought the sad victim tagalong story. I shook my head, then looked at the floor. "Right," he said. "Thoughts?"

The silence spun out. Then Nathan spoke again. "Don't we have a Sawzall in the machine shop?" There was a murmur. A couple of guys chuckled. "Seems like a good project for Ezekiel," Nathan continued. "He can put the truck pieces with the fertilizer bags. Judah can bury them too." He looked directly at Big John. "It's not like you have something better to do. 'A man reaps what he sows. Whoever sows to please their flesh, from the flesh will reap destruction.' Right, Ezekiel? Time to sow to please the Spirit." He sat back down. Big John looked angry, but I thought Nathan had done him a favor. Obviously, this community required atonement for something. At least he had a way to perform it.

Peter rubbed his hands together. "Good. Ezekiel will dismantle the truck. Judah will bury the pieces. The very small pieces." A pause. "And the trailer too. I assume we can't get that clean enough to save? No sparks, though, please, until the fertilizer has been transferred." He half smiled.

Big John would be a busy boy, I thought. And not much chance he'd be seen, alone in the Quonset for a month or twelve, sawing his Freightliner into penance shards. At least he'd be eating well.

Peter looked around. "That settles the immediate concerns," he said. "I'd like a further discussion just with family council." The men stood. Most of them headed toward the door. A few moved up to the front of the room. Big John, I noticed, held his seat.

I stood to leave. "You stay, if you would." Nathan spoke at my shoulder. He looked younger up close, more my age. He smiled at me. "We have some questions, and Ezekiel's answers last night were . . . a little fuzzy. We're hoping you might bring clarity." He was tall like the others but graceful. I could imagine him twenty years on, his face more weathered and his frame worn leaner from hard work and righteous living. For no reason, I was sorry I wouldn't see him to know if I'd guessed right.

I followed him to the front of the room. Someone had pulled chairs into a circle: seven, plus an extra for the girl guest. Big

John stayed off to the side. The men stood. They prayed. I bowed my head and watermeloned silently. I saw Nathan watching me. He caught my eye and raised an eyebrow. Possibly a lip-reader. Awesome. Then everyone sat and looked to Peter. Peter looked at me. "Ezekiel has told us," he began, "that you released him from a terrible bondage. He told us the government had blackmailed him into working undercover to entrap a terrorist group that planned to build a bomb." He was watching my face as he spoke. It did sound a little over-the-top, in that plain sunny room with breakfast smells still hanging in the air. I shrugged. That part wasn't my story. "He says he picked you up in Sacramento, that you were in trouble, running from someone, and wanted a ride to Cheyenne. Have I got this right so far?" I nodded. "Then somewhere along the line, you somehow deduced his problem and decided to solve it. This part of the story is unclear, both in the how and the why."

"It's horseshit," muttered Nathan. Big John's face was hard and blank. He sat in his chair staring down at his boots. I was on my own.

Peter looked at me. "Ezekiel told us that you altered the tracking device on his truck to misreport his location long enough for you both to get away. Is that true?"

"It's impossible!" Nathan exploded. "He's insulting our intelligence." He looked at Big John. "How do you think the combines navigate, Ezekiel? Or don't you think about that? We aren't plowing with oxen. We've advanced since you took off. We understand GPS." I knew that had been a dumb lie. Nathan turned to Peter. "I'm sorry." He looked at me. "It's Ruth, right? I'm sorry for interrupting. We'd just like the truth. Maybe you can tell us what you actually did. And why you did it."

Peter added, "Please."

"Yes," echoed Nathan. "Please."

I took a deep breath. "I can tell you what I did. Maybe that will help answer the why part too."

Nathan added, "This isn't an interrogation." Big John turned to watch me.

"That tracking unit on the truck was reporting back to a server in Homeland Security's Domestic Operations Center," I told them. "I copied the serial number off it. I assumed that was the identifier. I broke into the tracking server and modified the database so every unit in the region shared Big John's—" I caught myself. "Ezekiel's identifier. Then I made sure that the backup had my modified data. I crashed the server. By the time they got it restored and online, every target on the server shared our ID. It should have looked like we were everywhere. Then we got rid of the tracker."

Long silence. Peter looked at Nathan, the resident bullshit detector. Nathan was thinking through my story. He grinned. "And the government wants to lock you in a box? Surprising."

"Thank you," said Peter. "Is it the same people chasing you that are after Ezekiel?"

I shook my head. "I don't think so. I can't be sure. It could be different teams from the same agency."

"And do you share Ezekiel's belief that you have made a clean escape?"

I thought about it. I noticed they all wore some kind of hat. So the headscarf wasn't just to contain girl germs. The whole compound covered their heads. Except Big John. He'd lost his cap, and his bald head looked out of place. Maybe they hadn't let him into the special drawer yet. They were waiting on my answer. "For now, but they're really good at locating people. I told Ezekiel that. If there's ever been anything that placed him here, even twenty years ago, they'll find it." I studied Big John. Strangely, I was angry at him for risking these people. "A library fine, a speeding ticket, a second-place calf at the county fair, anything." They were watching me, and I was watching him. So I saw his face flicker. There was something, after all. They were coming for us.

Peter asked him, "Is there anything for them to find, Ezekiel?"

Big John shrugged. He was blank again. "Not that I remember."

Peter said to me, "Ezekiel claims they're more interested in you than in him."

"Then he knows more than I do." My stomach started to hurt. So that was the plan. "Follow my lead," Big John had said. That was going well. Now they would lay their hands on my head, send me as a scapegoat into the wilderness.

"It doesn't matter," said Nathan. "She's our guest, not collateral. She returned one of our own." He looked at Big John like he doubted the value of my effort.

Peter gazed thoughtfully at Nathan. The other men looked uncomfortable. "Ruth," he asked, "would you mind stepping out for a moment? This has turned into a family matter. You can wait just outside."

I walked to the door, and their eyes followed me. I wasn't invisible here. I went out into the kitchen. The room was empty, but there was work in progress: a pile of chopped carrots on the table, packages of meat defrosting by the sink, and four Instant Pots wheezing side by side. It smelled good, but I did not stop. I went outdoors and, keeping my head down, walked around the house to the open window where the men were arguing. I sat down on the grass to listen.

Big John was wound up. "The ram is given to die in Isaac's place!" he roared. "Abraham looked and lo in the thicket a ram caught by its horns. He took the ram and sacrificed it as a burnt offering in place of his son!" Traitor. I tried to remember he was desperate, but I was not inviting Big John to my birthday party.

"You self-serving shit." This was Nathan. "She's not some goat caught by the horns—she saved you. She's the Samaritan who gave aid when she could have passed by. We don't burn the Samaritan!"

It was Bible Death Bots. Peter stepped in. "That's enough. We need to do what best protects the community."

"How does sacrificing an innocent protect us?"

"She's no innocent." Big John, doubling down on shittiness.

"You don't actually know that."

"Enough!" A chair scraped. Peter was on his feet. "I'd like to discuss our choices like men. You can fight like boys afterwards, somewhere else." He cleared his throat. "So, one option, and I'm not endorsing it, is for Ezekiel to call his government contacts and negotiate an exchange: we trade Ruth for his immunity. He claims that would work. Thoughts?"

I had thoughts. So did Nathan. Obviously this family meeting was really a two-way rumble with Peter as judge and a crew of hat-packing extras. Nathan was trying to control his tone. "I don't think we can assess that without more information. What do they have on you, Ezekiel? You're saying she's a hotter target than you are for those guys, but why?" There was a long silence. And I wanted the answer as much as anyone in that room. But suddenly I remembered the phone. I'd given Big John the burner phone. So he could and surely would report me, no matter the decision. If he had the means to make the call. Would he have it with him? I thought maybe not. It was worth a try.

I crept back around the house and into the kitchen. Still empty. I hurried quietly up the stairs. The girls' dorm was to my left, so I turned right, down the hall. The men must sleep up here. I stepped through the door and looked into another dormitory. Twenty beds in five rows. Each had a small table and a drawer for storage underneath. I controlled my breathing, scanned the room. There would be a clue, there had to be. I forced myself to look at each bed, and finally I saw it, peeking out of the drawer: the top of a Spitz bag. Big John had stashed his snacks. I rushed over, pulled out the drawer, and rooted through it. Yes! I grabbed the phone and shoved it into my pocket. I pushed the drawer shut. And then of course I heard footsteps, heavy ones, coming up the stairs. I'd been only a few minutes ahead of him.

It might have been wiser to hide in the shower, but I loathe that scene where our heroine, frozen, holds her breath as the villain comes closer and closer. I only knew I wanted to meet him in a public space. I ran out of the dorm and straight into Big John as he came down the hallway. We faced each other.

"What were you doing in there?" he asked. I saw that he knew. His lips were nearly white.

"How could you?" I asked. I could hear the other men downstairs in the kitchen. In a moment, they would hear us as well. "How could you? You said to have faith. You said God would protect us."

"You don't believe that." Big John stepped toward me.

I braced myself. I was going to have to make him grab me.

"Give it back."

"No."

"GIVE. IT. BACK."

I moved to push past him, and he grabbed my arm. I screamed. He let go, and there was a rush of boots up the stairs. Nathan first, then Peter, with more men behind. I held my arm tight against me. I said nothing. I stared at Big John and let tears slide silently down my face. Take that, asshole.

"What is happening?" Peter put his hand hard on Big John's shoulder. "Ezekiel? What have you done?"

Nathan reached a hand out. "Ruth? Did he hurt you? Come out of there."

I didn't take his hand. Sideways, I stepped around Big John. "Get me away from him." I didn't offer an excuse for having been in the men's dorm. I let the drama carry me downstairs.

I heard Big John saying, "This is a misunderstanding." He wasn't going to tell them about the phone, and he wasn't quick enough to come up with something else. "I startled her, that's all. I swear it."

Peter said, "I think it's time for you to make a start on that semi. Get out of the house for a bit."

"We're making a mistake," said Big John. But he came down the stairs and, never looking at me, stomped out the door toward the Quonset, his shoulders slumped. I watched him go. I'd take him down now, if I could, but I was starting to like some of his people.

Nathan took a chair next to me. "What happened with Ezekiel up there?" he asked. His voice was kind, but the look was shrewd. I'd have to be careful lying to him.

"Last night, I loaned him a phone to call you guys. I decided I'd better get it back, and he caught me." The pile of cut carrots still sat there on the table, and I wondered what would happen if I started eating them. "The people after me," I said. "They don't want my head. They want what's inside it."

"So we can't just kill you and drop off your body?" said Nathan. "Good tip. Thanks."

I pulled the burner out of my pocket and set it in front of him. He didn't pick it up. He looked at it, and I wanted to ask: Did he have a phone? Did he have friends who sent him stupid tractor videos? An Instagram account?

"Keep that out of sight," he told me. "Mostly we don't have phones here." He turned to me. "It's not prison. It's a working farm, and that's how the work gets done." I probably looked skeptical. "You're right," he said. "There's more to it. But I don't think your mind needs my protection." He shrugged. "If it does, I'm not up to the job."

I put the phone back in my pocket. The woman called Deb came in the door. She greeted Nathan and smiled at me. I decided she was Nathan's mother. She went over to the Instant Pots and started doing meal-prep things. I watched her and thought how much I liked people who made me food. She was probably the biscuit baker. No chance she was an evildoer.

"Take a walk?" he asked me. "I have a couple more questions, if you're up to it."

"Dinner in an hour," said Deb.

"You can leave that bag," he told me. "No one will get into it."

I put it over my shoulder and followed him out. It was a clear morning and hot, my daylight introduction to Idaho. If I'd been forced to name three things about that state, I'd have said jagged mountains and clear streams through high meadows cross fenced with rustic buckrail. Pressed for the third item, I might have kept hate camps to myself and gone with wolves. Jerome was not that Idaho. Big John had brought us to the flatlands, bleak and arid.

Nathan led me past the Quonset. I saw that the driveway continued on past a series of neat metal outbuildings and a large poured-concrete pad with an overhead waterspout and racks of sprayer heads: the bomb dilution station. A sprayer rig crouched on the pad like a huge insect. We followed the road and came to three tiny houses set side by side, and then four modular homes spaced further apart. He paused. "Married couples live here, with their children." There was a small playground with swings and slides and some of the fun old-fashioned rides that made you barf or break your arm if you let go. Three long clotheslines stretched between metal Ts set in concrete. There was a washhouse off to one side, and I could see two women inside sorting through laundry and chatting, heads uncovered.

"Where are the kids?" I asked him. I wasn't sure what day of the week it was.

"School," he said. "Not here. They take the bus into Jerome."

"Really? They go to public school?"

"Yes," he told me. "Really. We let them out."

I didn't bother saying I hadn't meant that. We both knew I had. The road continued in a long dirt loop past round fields of alfalfa and what must have been the young barley, green under the huge irrigation pivots. After days of sitting, it felt good to be on my feet outdoors. I felt like a person, like I might have a normal day. Not my normal, of course, but religious hickabilly normal. Everywhere we passed pipes and pumps and small ponds to move or hold water. The last pivot wasn't running; there were people moving along it, doing repairs or maintenance. I saw Hannah and some of the other women from the dorm. They were working alongside the men, passing parts and tools. I saw Hannah notice me and then Nathan. She waved and bent to say something to the woman next to her. Everyone stopped to watch us walk on along the road toward a low rise.

"What was that?" I asked.

"Nothing," he answered. I walked on silently, and he added, "Gossip, I guess. We don't get so many new faces."

"Ezekiel's face isn't new."

"No."

"Did he tell you how he got in trouble?"

"No." Nathan sounded troubled. "Did he tell you?"

"No," I said. But I was starting to have a feeling about it. The longer Big John kept silent, the shorter my list of possibilities became.

"Peter will get it out of him eventually. It must be something really bad," said Nathan.

I mentally handed him a bronze No Shit Award.

"Look," he went on, "I want to ask you stuff, but I don't want to push you to where you're lying to me."

I stopped walking and faced him. "You could avoid that by not asking. We can talk about other things. I'll tell you what matters for you here. But maybe don't ask about me. You don't need to know any of that."

"I feel like I do," he said. He turned and pointed back where we'd been. I could see all the pivots, round and green, and the little community beyond them. I tried to guess what it all had cost, the land and water and equipment. There was money here, a lot of it, in a shape I hadn't seen before. Some kind of hawk spiraled up, harassed by smaller black birds. The breeze lifted my headscarf. "Here it is," Nathan said softly. "They call this area the Magic Valley, did you know that? Because of what irrigation and farming brought to the desert. We have more fields further away, but this is the main part. This is home."

I saw that word meant something to him, something like the word "money" meant to me: safety, purpose, the right kind of choices, good food. I looked where he pointed. I felt like I should comment, but only stupid stuff came to mind. "Nice," or "so green." Things you might also say about money. "Tell me about you," I said instead, "unless that puts you in the lying place."

"Clean shot." He chuckled. He stomped dust off his shoes and told me: born in Boise, overdosed mom and missing dad, he'd come as a foster to the farm at eight years old and never left. So that was the connection between us, I thought, watching the others stack tools carefully in the back of one of the pickups; it was orphan Doppler, reflecting back off a familiar broken surface. "Peter and Deb raised me as their own," he told me. "Ezekiel and I grew up together." So maybe not entirely familiar.

I looked at him. "You two are brothers."

"I guess." He was watching the trucks now too. One had turned up the road and was coming toward us. It was almost dinnertime. "There was always something off about Ezekiel."

"They'll come here after him." I wasn't guessing. Suddenly it seemed urgent. I imagined black choppers filling that quiet sky, armored vehicles crowding the dirt loop road. "He lied when he said there was nothing to find."

"I'm sure he did," said Nathan. "Any thoughts on what to do about that?"

Then the truck pulled up, Hannah driving. "Ride service!" she announced brightly. She pushed open the driver's door and slid across to the passenger seat.

Nathan climbed in. He looked at me. "Mind the tailgate?"

I shrugged. I was passing through. No catfights. I sat on the tailgate and rode down backward, wondering what was for dinner.

41

MIKE

FAILURE FIRST, THEN COLLABORATION

I t was 1600 hours before LuAnn, Gary, and Earl were back in San Francisco. By then, it was clear the truck had left the map, along with Homeland's undercover agent and Ruth. The open questions—why, how, and where, maybe who—demanded what Gary referred to as "interagency collaboration at the highest level." That translated to a single interminable meeting, with people shuffling in and out as updates trickled in. We were in some kind of surveillance war room. There were all the screens and cables and keyboards we could ever need.

After the various briefings, LuAnn shared a brief summary: her agent had last checked in from Winnemucca by phone. He'd been sick all day but had decided in the late afternoon to head for Laramie. He had not mentioned Ruth, but had said everything was on track. His truck had left Winnemucca and proceeded normally via Interstate 80 to the Sinclair at Elko, where it had pulled off, idled briefly, and then, unusually, shut down for almost ten minutes. After that, it had idled in Elko for more than two hours. LuAnn speculated their man might have had another round of illness. They had expected him to leave Elko and spend his mandatory rest period near Laramie, proceeding to Cheyenne (less than an hour's drive further) the next day. The truck had, as far as they knew, still been in Elko when the San Francisco tracking server had crashed. Staff had taken several hours to restore it, only to find the agent's ID replicated seven hundred times across their monitoring area. Ops staff were still manually repopulating the database, but it was apparent the tracker on the agent's rig was no longer operational. The truck itself had vanished, along with the agent and our asset.

"What about the targets in Cheyenne?" Gary was trying to add value.

"They waited several hours past the scheduled meetup and then dispersed. We're monitoring them, of course, but they seem unlikely to have choreographed this disappearance. They could have intercepted the truck, but they lack the ability to interfere with the server, as far as we know."

"And the driver?" Gary was just making her hop, but I wanted to hear this part.

LuAnn picked up her legal pad and checked her notes. "Ezekiel Archibald Arnold," she said. "Thirty-nine years old, born in Twin Falls, Idaho. Pretty thin background on him, it turns out. Freelance owner-operator of a Class 8 Freightliner. We caught him several years ago on interstate trafficking of minors for the purpose of prostitution and associated revolting acts. He had three girls and two boys shackled in his trailer, all under fourteen years old. He signed on to the bomb sting to stay out of prison." She set the pad down. "It was not my call to cut a deal with him. That would not have been my choice. Anyhow, that's all I have on him so far."

Earl had been sitting quietly, but now he sat up. "Could he have pulled this off, do you think?"

"He could have driven the truck," LuAnn said. "The planning and technical work would have to be another party. Ours is not a sophisticated individual, and this escape had to be planned well in advance." Earl caught my eye. "And you boys can stop ogling each other," she said. "If your target fits the profile for any of this operation, it's past time to speak up."

I hadn't seen Gideon come in, but now he spoke from the back of the room. "Our asset is an unknown for the server hack, if it was a hack. She has advanced microchip skills but has relied on others previously for basic software development."

LuAnn thought about that answer. "Are you suggesting the server crash and database corruption could be a coincidence or unrelated to the truck disappearance?"

Gideon hesitated. Was he formulating an evasion, I wondered, or just framing his answer carefully? "Every conclusion leads to complications," he said at last. "It looks most like a hack. A random crash should have left log entries and more general data corruption. We would see a CPU panic or memory errors or something. And the backup should not have been affected." He rubbed his forehead. "That said, a deliberate, complex intervention behind our firewall at the exact time two people of interest to two different agencies were about to disappear in Elko, Nevada . . ."

LuAnn frowned. Gary looked lost. Earl was clicking his pen—in, out, in, out. He spoke up. "An inside job? Are you suggesting someone internal here hacked that server in coordination with those two?"

Gideon made a vague gesture. "I can't rule it out." His tone changed. "Can you?"

"I'm not the tech expert." Earl was irritated. "I don't know a fucking thing about what went on with that server." He set down his pen. "Mike? What do you think? You've followed Ruth the longest. Is this part of something larger on our side?"

I had in front of me sixty-five pages of printed acquisition records that were damning and, likely, incomplete proof of something larger. Because I'm a record keeper, I also had a copy of my initial prohibition of those purchases. I was still convinced that Ruth could not be involved in any complex, widespread compromise. She was a rule breaker, yes, but she was *my* rule breaker; I had taken that terrible sales job to restrict her impact to domestic banks. Someone else had placed Ruth's chip in our networks without my knowledge and also, I thought, without hers. Someone else must have realized her predicament in Elko and broken into that server to free her. But who was that person? And, I had to admit to the hole in my defense.

How would Ruth have known to run, if she were not involved? Why did that truck go off course right then, if she were oblivious to the Homeland compromise? I looked around the room; Earl, Gideon, Gary, and LuAnn looked back at me. Someone knew more than I did. Very likely that someone was in the room. To tip my hand now would be a risk. "No," I said. "I have no knowledge of anything larger."

Earl retrieved his pen. "Well," he said (click, click, click), "until we learn something to the contrary, I think the simplest explanation should guide us here."

"Which one is that?" Gary, grasping for comprehension.

Earl smiled without humor. "Yeah, good question: Which one is that? My vote, for the sake of formal logic, is to avoid the proliferation of hypothetical villains. We blame someone we know exists." No doubt, we were getting our money's worth out of his contract. How else to arrive at the damn obvious?

"So it was Ruth?" said Gary.

I had to say something. "But why would it be Ruth? She could just have got off that truck and disappeared. Why would she protect a child sex trafficker, one hauling a bomb? And how did she get through to that server in the first place? If she hired someone for scripting, how did she pull off a database hack?"

"Also good questions," said Earl. "But what we have right now are probabilities. What is more likely: that Ruth is mysteriously capable and has murky motives, or that we have a secret super-saboteur in our midst?" He was persuasive, in an alliterative way.

"Could it be both?" asked Gary.

Earl sighed loudly. I mentally stuffed his company's sugges-
tion box with a manners class. "Yes, sir. It *could* be both, but
that's improbable. I'm trying to go with the most likely explanation, not the least likely one." Gary subsided into mute con-
fusion. I put my hand reflexively over my pile of papers. I had a
different calculus on the likelihood of a second and more malevolent bad guy.

LuAnn spoke. "So you guys are suggesting that your target
engineered the escape of our guy, for reasons unknown. Have I
got that right?"

"It's a working hypothesis," said Earl.

"She works for the terrorists? For the sex traffickers? Both?"

"No," I said, and Earl, and Gideon, all of us together.

"Ah," she said. "One point of agreement, at least."

Gary sat up. He elaborately checked his watch. "Apologies,"
he said. "I need to cut this short. Earl? Gideon? I need to brief
the director. I'd like you two to join me, in case he needs elabo-
ration on any details." The three of them made a noisy exit.

LuAnn started to gather her things. "I guess that's the meeting," she said.

I took a breath. Here was one person in the hierarchy I felt I
could trust. "Ma'am." I picked up my stack of papers. "Can you
spare a minute? We have a complication."

She set down her bag. "I'll make you a trade. You read me in
on your target—what she did and why she matters—and I'll
hear you out on your complication."

"Our complication."

"Whatever."

"It's a deal." I looked around the room. There was network infrastructure everywhere. "But we need to talk outside."

"In the SCIF?"

"No," I decided. The classified briefing room might be packed with bugs. "In the park. You'll understand. Humor me."

We went downstairs and crossed the street. Out of sight of any windows, away from any blinking box, we sat on a peeling bench, and I told LuAnn the story of Ruth. I handed her my pile of acquisitions records that showed, in a rough way, the extent of our injury, as well as my single failed attempt to prevent it.

She paged through the records. Then she sat without moving for seven minutes. I could tell she was reviewing what she'd learned, organizing the information, integrating it with whatever else she knew that I did not. "I wonder," she mused, "who that girl might have become, without your interference."

She waited, and I realized she expected a response. "Well—" I paused. I hadn't asked myself the question in that way. "Probably nobody. Most nineteen-year-olds have more potential than body hair, but nothing comes of it." I sensed her disbelief, and added, without reflection, "I myself was thought to have great potential at one time. In fact, I was a Rhodes Scholarship finalist."

"I don't know what that is." She picked up her briefcase and stood to go. "And I've seen your file. 'Potential' is not the word for it." She added, over her shoulder, "If you worked for me, I'd fire you. What a fucking shit show." But I was glad I'd told her.

42

SECONDS

Dinner was burgers and a side they called salad that was horribly sweet. It had carrots, raisins, green Jell-O, and a lot of white nondairy filler that was probably Cool Whip. I wanted to like it. I wanted to like everything produced in that kitchen. I failed but ate it anyhow. The Clean Plate Club was not elective here.

Big John didn't come in to eat. Peter was late. I saw him walking up from the Quonset, looking frustrated and angry. After I finished and cleared my place, I took a second plate and dressed another burger with pickles and a large pile of onions. I scooped a helping of the carrot mixture onto the side and headed quietly to the door. As I pushed it open, I caught Deb's eyes following me. I stopped. She nodded her head: go on. So I went.

Big John was leaning against the semi tractor, his back to the door. He was making noise with a mallet—banging away at the bumper. In geologic time, it could have contributed to the deterioration of the vehicle. Maybe. He didn't notice me come in. I walked around in front of him and waited.

He stopped hammering. "You."

I offered him the plate. He considered it, then set his sledge on the hood and took the food. "I don't suppose you remembered a fork?"

I had not.

"Or a napkin?"

I shook my head.

"Oh well." He scooped up some of the salad with his fingers. "I missed this stuff. I know you're meant to come home for family, but I missed the salad more. I've had better burgers out there, but Mom's salad is the best."

I leaned against the bench. Again, I watched him eat. He finished the carroty glop before he started on the burger. Dessert first. I looked around the shop. I located the laptop almost right away, plugged in and open on a metal welding table against the wall. He'd obviously been trying to log into it. I'd disabled the cellular link and changed the password when I finished with it in Winnemucca. A good move.

Big John followed my look. He wiped his mouth. "Yeah," he said. "I tried that too." He sounded almost cheerful. "Nothing personal."

"Why me?"

"I wish it wasn't." He set the empty plate down behind him. "I actually like you, Ruth. You're a tough girl, and you saved me when you didn't have to. But getting me home isn't enough. I need an offering, a substitute, to cleanse my particular sins. Like when Abraham is told to sacrifice Isaac but gets around it? Nathan says you aren't that offering, but he's soft about women."

"Why don't you just come clean? Your dad seems ready to forgive anything."

"Ah well." Big John flexed his hands. His voice was grim. "So he says. But if I tried it, we would see at once the limits of Peter's forgiveness. Sorry to disappoint you." He looked up. "I have not been a good man, Ruth. But God has set me above you, and He has shown me a way to go on. I didn't choose you, just as Abraham did not choose the ram. You were placed here by God."

"I guess we'll find out."

He smirked at me. "All I need is a five-minute phone call. You think I can't make that happen?" He held out the plate. "Here. Thanks for lunch. Tell Mom I liked the salad."

I took his dirty dish. He was watching, so I did not also take the laptop. I did count my steps past it to the door, in case I could come back after dark.

I met Peter as I walked to the house. He indicated the plate. "Did Deb send you with that?"

"No."

He sighed. "Why do women use food to convey forgiveness?" Then he smiled at me. I heard the pounding restart in the Quonset. "Don't worry. I'm not angry. You have a right. And yours may be the wiser path."

I decided not to tell him that forgiveness had no part in my meal delivery. I'd taken the food to scout the laptop.

Peter turned to go. "I believe Nathan was hoping you might look at the calibration software for the sprayer. Have a good afternoon." He nodded at me and went on down toward the banging.

Nathan was waiting, but he didn't mention the sprayer. "Let's go for a drive," he said. We took one of the white pickups. I tossed my bag on the floor, rolled down the window, and hung my arm out. I should have been planning the next stage of my escape. I should have been stealing the laptop and hoarding leftover biscuits. I wondered if I was repeating whatever miscalculation had made me overstay my safety in California.

"Do you have family somewhere?" Nathan asked.

I eyed him across the truck. "No."

"Just no? No one at all?"

"Are you planning to hold me for ransom?"

"Of course not, no. I've told you, you're safe with me." He had turned toward Jerome. We passed other farms, some with big blue silos. We passed hundreds, maybe thousands, of black-and-white cows crowding long cement feed bunkers. Everywhere, I saw green irrigation ponds and big sprinkler systems. I smelled manure and dust. Then Nathan was navigating us through town. It had wide streets scattered with low boxy buildings. There was a lot of asphalt, and why not? The pavement was likely prettier than the ground it covered. He pulled into a

Dairy Queen. "How about a Blizzard? Give you something to remember when you're rotting in our dungeon."

"I'd love one. But I should stay in the truck." It was weird how much I wanted to get out, order at the counter, sit in a booth or under the spindly tree out front. I reminded myself I wasn't ready to die, not for low-dairy soft serve.

He blinked, then said, "Crap, right. I forgot you're a wanted mass murderer or something. Better wait here. What can I get you?"

"The Heath. Please."

"Edgy," he said.

"Let me pay for it." I reached for some cash.

"Come on, now." He grinned at me as he got out of the truck. "Leave me my pride. We can pretend I'm thanking you for bringing my long-lost brother home, if you want."

"OK," I said. I adjusted my headscarf. Just a nice girl out for an ice cream with her upstanding guy.

Nathan drove us out to another of their pivots. There was no shade. We sat against the truck tires with our shakes. Some of the alfalfa was starting to bloom, and the air was sweet as bees buzzed among the flowers. It was absurdly bucolic. I reminded myself to straighten up and stay alert. I plopped imaginary Hydrant Mikes around the field. I gave him tactical gear and a gun, but it wasn't his look.

"So what's your next move, Ruth? Are you headed somewhere in particular? Is there someone waiting for you?" Nathan twirled his straw. He'd ordered peanut butter cup, the flavor choice of a middle schooler.

"My next move is to eat this thing," I said.

"Come on."

"I won't answer your questions, Nathan. Dangerous people might sit you in a room and ask about my plans. They'll sense it if you know."

He sighed. He stared at the pivot. I wondered what it looked like to a person who understood every part. Maybe he was disassembling it in his head, servicing whatever needed it, replacing worn bits. Or maybe he wasn't seeing the pivot and was thinking silly thoughts about me. He said, "How old are you, Ruth? Can you tell me that?"

"Twenty-six."

He nodded. "I'll be thirty next month. I've been farming here my whole life. And I'm good at it. I like it. There's always something to do." He turned toward me. "But, I don't know if this makes sense to you, there's also nothing to do. I love my work and my people, but I look around sometimes, and it feels like there's nothing happening. Can you understand that?" I thought the ugly landscape and God stuff must make it extra boring, but I did understand him. He read that in my face and went on. "Now you show up and suddenly something is happening. Something interesting and important. But you're just going to leave. You'll disappear, and I won't even know what happens to you."

I had no answer for that either. I watched a bee crawl across my Walmart sneaker and felt oddly sad. I'd known him less than a day.

He asked, "When you're praying, what are the words? Is it Hebrew?"

"It's watermelon," I told him. "I don't pray. I just repeat the word 'watermelon.' Ezekiel said I should bow my head and move my lips here." I saw him think about that. We sat a long time without speaking. No matter what imaginary threats I spread through the alfalfa, I felt safe with him. Maybe because Nathan didn't know me or, worse, because he somehow did. I made a silent list of things we couldn't talk about. I imagined long years with a man who mixed mayonnaise in his ketchup and called it "fry sauce." I thought about real coffee, and complicated restaurant food, and $225 million. Then I gave up and rested there in a feeling I didn't recognize and couldn't keep. I stored it away like the smell of new doughnuts or a fiddle tune that fades from your ear.

Finally Nathan got to his feet. He crumpled his empty cup and held his hand out to help me up. "We'd better get back. Mom will want us on time to supper."

I don't remember what we ate. Big John didn't appear and neither did Peter. I watched for them until very late. I was hoping to sneak down to the Quonset for the laptop, but they never came out.

43

MIKE

A PIN IN THE MAP

We had our second cross-agency collaborative update at 2200 hours. LuAnn presented photos of her driver from the cash register camera at the Winnemucca Sinclair. She tapped the pull-down screen with a blue Montblanc rollerball. (My father was a collector of midrange luxury writing implements; I inherited his interest, but not his financial resources. I'm thus forced to rely on a standard government-issue Skilcraft medium ballpoint in black.) "He paid cash for his food and his fuel. That's a first. And we think he stayed in the lot for at least two hours afterwards." She tucked the pen behind her ear. "This is a large man with a history of violence. We can't overlook the possibility that he discovered your girl's skills and coerced her to help him. That may be more likely than her finding common cause with a sex trafficker and engineering a joint escape. We have no record of her outside that truck since Sacramento, is that right?"

Earl sat in front. He offered, "She'd have known to dodge the cameras."

"Sure," said LuAnn. "That's possible." She looked at him. "Any thoughts on what she's up to, then?"

"No," Earl replied, "and I also don't know if or how she broke into your server. But"—and his eyes flicked my way—"I do think we need to be careful attributing too much strategy to her choices." LuAnn waited. He continued. "She strikes me as impulsive under pressure. She's bright but she's improvising. Like that move she pulled on the fire alarm in the Ops Center? No way that was planned. She got stuck in the wrong place and found a clever way out. If she'd really had a plan, she wouldn't have been there in the first place."

"Fair enough. So you're saying she got a hunch it wasn't safe to go to Cheyenne? And then, what, broke through our firewall, blew up our server, and hijacked a truck bomb rather than just getting out and hiding in the women's room?"

Earl looked embarrassed. "It seems less likely when you put it that way."

I asked, "How much tech was on the truck?"

"He had the normal commercial GPS, a secondary tracking unit wired to a battery, and an in-cab camera. Along with a laptop and a phone that have also stopped reporting."

"Ruth wouldn't have missed all of that." As I spoke, I remembered everything she'd missed in her own apartment and personal effects. Surely, she was more alert now, out on her own.

"So we're back to Earl's hypothesis that Ruth disappeared the truck and driver, now updated to stipulate that she did so on impulse?"

Earl said, "I realize how that sounds."

"Do you? And how are you explaining her server access?"

Earl said, "I can't. It's not my skill set, like I said. But I bet someone can tell us how it was done, eventually. I doubt it's impossible."

LuAnn looked around the room. "Does anyone have anything better than Earl's Magic 8 Ball stuff? Something tangible? Actionable?"

There was a shuffling sort of silence. Then Gideon spoke. "I think I know where they went." He walked to the front of the room. He handed her a small stack of printouts.

"What's this?" LuAnn studied a photo.

"This is the truck leaving the Elko Sinclair. It's from their security camera. You can see most of the front plate there, and the driver's face. Sort of."

She looked closer. "Probably him. I can have our facial recognition team verify it. What are the rest of these?" She flipped through more pictures, all road views at night.

Gideon stepped around to stand next to her. "These are stills from Idaho traffic cameras. I can walk you through my analysis, but I'm confident he turned north off I-80 at Wells. The Idaho cameras are focused on southbound traffic, unfortunately, but these are a couple partials of your truck's rear plate as it headed north on Highway 93."

I had to admire Gideon's impulse control, waiting for each of us to look stupid before his big reveal. In the last day he had somehow found and tracked the rig. Meanwhile Homeland was still dusting Twinkies for prints in Elko, and I had a pile of vaguely incriminating database records. Gideon had lapped us.

LuAnn set down the photos. "So where's he going? Why Idaho?"

Gideon flourished his last piece of paper. "You were right that your driver is basically a ghost. But I did find this. I think he's going home." He set down a blurry newspaper clipping.

By now we had all gathered around LuAnn. We examined Gideon's prize. The clipping was a photo from *The Denver Post* dated January 7, 1981. In it, a chubby boy clutched a massive trophy. The caption read "Five-year-old Ezekiel Arnold of Jerome, Idaho, lands on top in the annual National Western Stock Show Mutton Busting."

Gary focused immediately on the least important element. "Mutton busting?"

LuAnn answered, maybe with pity. "They sit little kids on sheep and turn them loose. The longest ride wins." She considered the photo. "It's bull-rider kindergarten. They wear helmets now." She asked Gideon, "Where is Jerome, relative to Boise?"

Gideon consulted his phone. "It's southeast on 84 by 116 miles, according to Google." He shrugged. "South central Idaho? It's agricultural flatlands. I really don't know the place."

Earl said, "What an incredible find, Gideon. What led you

to that particular edition of *The Denver Post*? This is amazingly fast work."

Gideon regarded him steadily. "I cast a wide net. Why?"

"Just impressed," said Earl, adding in a mumble, "and pretty fucking curious."

LuAnn ignored Earl. "So you think he's headed back to Jerome? He has people there?"

"I'm not sure. There are Arnolds living outside the town. At least, I found their names on a couple of titles, big agricultural parcels. Farmers, I think." Gideon added, "You did say he wasn't a genius."

"OK," LuAnn said. "Thank you. And well done. You're a miracle worker." Her tone was flat. She picked up his papers. "I'm teaming you with Earl and Mike for the next phase. No more solo flights."

Gideon opened his mouth, certainly to object.

"Don't make me find you in an org chart." She turned toward the others in the room. "I want addresses, names, ages, for every person at every address where he might be. We don't set foot on-site until we know what we're doing and who's involved. I mean it, no dead babies or burning buildings. Of course, that fucker would bury himself in civilians. At least he's probably planning to stay put."

Gary was still awake. "I'm afraid I need to flex my arm here. We have an asset in the wind."

LuAnn looked at him.

I heard Earl mutter, "Giddyup."

"I beg your pardon?"

"I said"—Gary got louder—"we have an asset . . ."

"I heard you. In the wind. In the American wind, as far as we know. On the domestic lam. I am giving you a chance to stop talking."

"Um." I think Gary was trying to stop but could not find the brake. Like some demented geezer, he stomped the verbal gas and drove straight through the plate-glass window trying to park at the Dunkin'. Or maybe he couldn't stand a woman telling him what to do. He kept talking. "It's a little late for niceties. We need to find this girl before she's taken by a hostile power and destroys the worldwide internet. This is bigger than your little sparkler party."

I swear I saw her squint her left eye before she dropped her scope on the past-its-prime bull that had stumbled into the clearing beneath her blind. This time, Gary was worth the ammo. "Have it your way," she said. "I officially claim sole jurisdiction over this operation. You are relieved of all duties. I want every relevant record in my possession within the hour. Your staff reports to me or they're out." She looked around. We all got busy acting busy. "Looks like they're staying."

Gary didn't move. I think he was wondering who'd been running his mouth.

"OK, old man," she offered. "I'll help you out." She took his arm by the elbow and hooked it expertly over her shoulder. With all of us intently not watching, she maneuvered him to the doorway and, with a light shove, sent him off down the hall.

"Damn," sighed Earl.

LuAnn spoke to us from the door. "I'm going to update my

boss," she said. "I want us on the ground in Idaho in twenty-four hours, tops. Do what you need to do." She followed Gary down the hall.

"Wow," continued Earl.

"About time," added Gideon.

I asked, "Who here thinks Ruth is in Idaho?"

"Not me," volunteered Earl. "I can't see her taking that ride. I assume she traded that server trick to get out of the truck. She's . . . somewhere else. Gone to ground again."

Gideon was frowning. "I want to say no, but I'm not sure. I feel like something may have happened." We looked at him. He grimaced. "I'm assuming they have her."

"They?" There was an edge to Earl's voice. Gideon heard it, of course.

"Yes, 'they.' Third person plural for the Christian nutters hiding Homeland's sex felon bomb driver."

"You didn't mention the Christian nutter part to LuAnn."

"I didn't?" He was unbothered. "Long night. And it's all guess-work, really. Idaho demographics. Might be LDS instead, but I don't think so."

"So how do we figure it out?" I wanted to kick them both, but I was learning to accept a certain quota of assholes in every room. "How do we find Ruth?"

Gideon said, "If they have her, and she's alive, they should make contact soon to negotiate. They won't wait for the helicopters."

He saw my face.

"What, Mike, don't tell me you haven't thought it. You had

to know this wouldn't end with her in your kitchen making soup and macramé owls."

"Lots of possibilities between macramé owls and death by Bible thumpers," said Earl. "Let's just hope she's alive." He looked at Gideon. "Want to bet on it? It's midnight now. How long until they make that call?"

"Sure," Gideon said. "Why not? Twenty-four hours. If I win, you don't speak for two days."

Earl could take an insult—he probably had practice. "Deal. And if I win, I get the call history off that phone in your pocket." It was a surprising ask, and interesting. They glared at each other.

"Great," I said. "Good talk, guys." For something to do, I pulled up a map of Jerome. Where was she?

44

RUTH

JUDGMENT, OR
SOMETHING LIKE IT

I got up at dawn that second morning. I showered and dressed as quietly as I could and carried my bag down to the kitchen. I'd decided to be gone before supper. I had no idea when or how I would leave, or where I would go. I would make it happen. I had no business with these people. I sensed pursuers on my trail, snouts down, seeking blood. I sat a few minutes at the table before Deb came in, pulling on her apron and lighting the gas under the kettle before she reached for the light switch.

"Oh!" She steadied herself. "I didn't see you there. Is everything OK?"

Something difficult hung between us. I was the younger woman who had returned one son broken and was interfering somehow with the other, not a Samaritan to Deb but a strange female power and an augury of pain. Deb was to me, more simply, someone else's mother; she was off-limits.

I said, "I was awake and thought you might want help with breakfast." I stopped. "That's not true. What I really wanted to ask, before I left, was if you'd teach me to make those biscuits."

Deb smiled. "I thought you liked those." She reached for a second apron. "Set that bag down where it won't get covered. Wear this. Now come around here and I'll show you." She pulled out a huge mixing bowl, dumped in flour, salt, and baking powder, and taught me how to cut cold butter into the flour mix with two opposing table knives. I cut, turned the bowl, cut again, turned the bowl. I paused. "What is it?" she asked. She was slicing meat, tactfully not hovering.

"It feels like there should be a tool for this job," I said, "for how often you do it."

She turned away toward the stove. "There is. I use my big food processor. But you won't have that, will you?" It was gently done. She didn't shove me out the door.

I kept cutting until she told me to stop. She stirred in cold milk, rolled out the dough, folded it a couple of ways, and showed me how to cut the biscuits without crushing the layers.

As her people started to come down for breakfast, I pulled a tray out of the oven. Deb looked over my shoulder, poked them critically, and said, "These are a fine start. You'll do even better with practice."

I didn't own two table knives, a sheet pan, or a kitchen to keep them in. But I thought when I had those things, I would remember Deb. I would bake my own good biscuits and share them with my old dog. I might buy a food processor.

Nathan found me sitting outside. "How about some bomb disposal?"

"OK," I agreed. "Seems like a useful life skill."

"For you, anyhow."

"Hey, now," I told him. "Not my terrorist plot."

He chuckled. "Born to trouble," he commented. "As the sparks fly upward."

We walked together down to the sprayer.

The ammonium nitrate was hard to deal with. Probably we got in a hurry and tried to use too much at once. Adding it to water made it really cold. We tried mixing it in the tank and froze a connector. Nathan warmed it with a torch, and a hose split. Then a thick layer of the granules precipitated to the bottom, threatening to clog the nozzles.

"Stop," Nathan said. "Hang on, let me think."

I'd already stopped. I'd been mostly useless anyhow. Strangely, my facility with microchips had failed to translate into mixing fertilizer.

Nathan looked in the bag. He pulled out a handful of the white, clumping material. He sniffed it.

"What's it smell like?"

"Hard to say." He was frowning.

"What's it meant to smell like?"

"I have no idea." He walked to the center of the driveway. "Bring me that torch." I handed it to him. He set the handful of white stuff on the ground, lit the torch, and pointed it. There was a flicker of flame. The small mound of fertilizer burned slowly, then fizzled out. He frowned more. He wet a finger, dabbed it in the pile, and carefully tasted it. "Huh." I decided to reserve my next stupid question. I waited. He said, "It acts like ammonium nitrate, kind of. The cold is right. But it doesn't burn like it should. I don't know the chemistry well enough. It's like it's been treated with something."

"So it couldn't make a bomb?"

"Doesn't seem like it. Not this bag, anyhow. And it's not dissolving properly in the tank."

I puzzled over that. If an unwilling undercover agent delivers a load of mysteriously denatured explosives to a domestic terror cell as part of a Homeland Security sting operation, what are the implications? I said, "I wonder what that means."

Nathan heard a different question. "It means we're not spraying this on the barley. I don't know what it is. Let's put these bags back in the trailer. Then we need to drive the sprayer over to the cleaning station. I'll show you how to wash it out."

Dinner that day was stew with meat and vegetables in a heavy broth. Deb served it over mashed potatoes in ceramic bowls. I didn't notice until I sat down that the other women had all declined the potatoes. Hannah, who ate next to me, looked at my bowl and said, "Oh, you'll love Deb's potatoes. I wish I could eat them but you know"—she rolled her eyes—"carbs."

They might not have phones or computers, or thoughts of their own, I decided, but they had modern diet lingo, and were spoiled about food.

"Of course," Hannah went on, "you're so skinny. I got stuck

with these curves." She flashed her eyes to the men's table as she said this. She hadn't liked seeing me again with Nathan. I could have reassured her I'd be gone soon and forever, but I didn't. And when I noticed some of the men going back for more, I also got seconds. I had no idea where I'd be in a day; surely no one would be mashing me potatoes.

Deb smiled when I returned with my bowl. "Take all you want," she said. "A cook loves an appetite." She touched my shoulder gently as I turned back to the table. Big John, I noticed, had still not come in. I wondered if starvation was part of Peter's plan to extract a confession, or if Big John was on a hunger strike. Even if they took me captive, I would not be hunger striking. Probably I'd spill my secrets first.

After dinner, Hannah took my hand. "Come help with the pivot! It will be fun." Which seemed unlikely.

Peter intercepted us at the door. "Sorry to steal your assistant, Hannah," he said. "I'll need Ruth this afternoon." Nathan hovered behind him.

Hannah saw him. "Fine." She dropped my arm. "Whatever." What amazing thing did she think we'd do without her? She needed a hobby.

Peter and Nathan and I went back into the room off the kitchen. "Sit, please," Peter instructed, so I sat. I noticed I was waiting to hear how I could help them. I wasn't planning my defense or my escape. I could be Esau, I realized, selling my birthright for a mess of potage. Two messes, I corrected: a Heath Blizzard and a lot of biscuits. I was not the cheapest date in the biblical world.

"I told him what you said yesterday," said Nathan. "That you thought Ezekiel had lied, and they would find him here."

Peter asked, "Are you sure?"

I said, "It was his expression when I listed things that might catch him out. He seemed like he remembered something. If it places him here, it doesn't matter what it was."

Nathan asked Peter, "Did he tell you what he did yet?"

"No." They glanced significantly at each other, the look of worldly men shielding a gentle female from their dark, dark thoughts.

I said, irritably, "If Homeland Security was blackmailing him, and it seems they were, you're almost certainly dealing with interstate trafficking of something seriously illegal. You already know about the explosives, and I think he would admit to drugs or guns. So, children for sex is top of the list." And immediately I wished I'd kept my mouth shut. They knew already, of course they knew, or guessed at least. Hearing me say it cut Peter right to his soul. The parable of the prodigal son drew a hard line at monetized child rape, apparently. He'd clung to the hope of something else, I saw, until I'd said the words aloud. "I could be wrong," I added weakly, but I could not unsay my guess.

"Dad?" said Nathan. "She can't be sure of that. It's just speculation."

"But she's probably right," said Peter. "We both know it." He closed his eyes and rested his head in his hands. I thought, belatedly, about the neat little playground and the kids who would be getting off the bus to play in it.

We sat quietly. Both men seemed to be praying. I thought about Deb making supper. I wondered what was on the menu. I needed to leave before I got more attached to the meal plan, or the cook. Peter asked me, "Do you have a way to find out exactly what Ezekiel did? I need to be certain."

I considered the problem. Would his arrest record be on a server somewhere that I could break into and search? I didn't know. Undercover agents must be protected from easy discovery. Gideon would know Big John's history by now, I was sure of that. I could call him and ask. But he would want something. And it would give up my location. I said, "I don't know if that information is anywhere I could find it. There's someone I could call, but it would confirm that I'm still with your son. It would make it more dangerous when they come."

Nathan said, "We can't ask her to take another risk for us. Can't you just finesse it somehow? Tell Ezekiel that you asked Ruth to clear him, and this is what she came back with?"

Peter looked at him. "You mean lie?"

"Well, rearrange the facts. To arrive at the truth."

"Two wrongs don't make a right, son."

"Stretching a story to protect our kids doesn't seem all that wrong to me."

Peter turned to me. "I don't play by your rules," I offered, "but you could bring him up here and let me tell him what I told you. See what happens." He hesitated. "If it doesn't work," I added, "I'll make the call. I can leave right after, tell them that I've gone."

"No," said Nathan. "You don't owe us that."

"We need the truth," Peter decided. "I won't sacrifice him until I'm sure." Nathan and I sat, wordless. "What did you think we were talking about?" Peter asked. "He can't be here if he did what she says, and they'll kill him in prison. I'll get him now. You two wait here." He left the room, and we heard the door slam behind him.

"I am so sorry," I told Nathan.

He shook his head. "You didn't do anything wrong. Dad's right, we need to know the truth. This is Ezekiel's path. He chose it." He paused, then rushed on. "We only have a couple of minutes. You need to let me speak. This timing is terrible, but I might not get another chance." I braced myself hard against whatever he was poised to say. He took a breath. "Ruth, stay. We can hide you. You have to stop running eventually, so stop now and stay with me. I don't care what you've done." He considered taking my hand, thought better of it. He met my blank look. "I'm worth changing plans for, Ruth. You and I could be worth that."

I stopped thinking about food. My head filled with all the ways he was wrong, but I managed not to say any of them. Of course he didn't care what I'd done; he didn't know what it was. Or who I was. My unsuitability for Nathan, for his pivots and prayers and mother with biscuits, that had started at conception and been compounded with every choice and chance event since then. It wasn't the moment to decide whether I minded, whether I wished I even had a choice beyond how to refuse. I swallowed and said, "Nathan, no. I can't stay. I don't belong here, and I won't bring more trouble to you or your people. But thanks for asking."

He opened his mouth to argue with me or to blurt more sad nonsense. Then we heard the front door open and close, and Peter brought Big John into the room and shut the door behind them. Saved by the felon.

Big John greeted us. "Oh, for fuck's sake," he said. His hands bled from a mosaic of jagged cuts. The Sawzall had been taking him to school. "Why are these two here?"

Peter directed him to a chair. He said, "Before we talk, I need you to give me your sidearm." Big John looked sulkily at him. "You lost control the other morning. You shamed yourself and embarrassed me. I won't permit you to threaten a woman here." Peter held out his hand.

The moment lengthened, and then Big John snorted. "Fine," he said. "Whatever you want. I see where I stand." He unbuttoned his shirt and unholstered his Ruger. Handed it to his father. "Here. Take it."

Peter examined the gun and placed it carefully on the table behind him. "I asked Ruth if she knew the specifics of how you came to be working undercover. I've asked her to repeat to you what she said to me and your brother." He turned to me.

Big John studied his hands. "Here we go," he said.

I faced him. "I told them it takes a really big interstate violation to get Homeland's attention. It's not explosives, you've already talked about that. And we all know you're not into drugs."

"Hell no," he muttered under his breath. "I don't do that shit."

"What about little kids, Ezekiel," I said. "You want to tell us how you do those?" He cringed like someone large had struck him. He started to sweat. I pressed him. "Why do you think I took that phone," I said. "You didn't ask yourself why I needed it so badly? Who I might call? What I might find out?" The silence was excruciating. I had to go on, I realized, until somehow he broke. "They gave me names, Ezekiel. The children's names. It's quite a list. Did you bother to learn them? Do you want to hear them now?"

Big John moaned. He fell forward hard onto his knees. "No," he mumbled. "No." He groveled and started to weep. He clutched at Peter, grabbed him around the legs. Tears and snot streamed down his face. "Dad," he whimpered, "Dad."

Peter looked down at his son. He crossed his arms. His face was twisted and terrible. "Confess," he said. "Confess to God, and to your father who raised you. Who took you in and defended you. Ezekiel!" He was shouting. "Confess!"

I looked away. I had no place here. I should not be watching. Quietly I raised myself out of my chair, thinking to slip out.

Nathan grabbed my arm. "Stay," he hissed. "You're part of this. Stay and bear witness."

Fuck that, I thought, but I sat back down.

The room had narrowed to Big John and his father and, it seemed, his angry God. The words stumbled out of him. "I tried not to do it," he whimpered. "I tried and tried. I struggled for so long. Why did you tempt me? Why? Why choose me for such a sin?" His eyes focused on Peter. "I did it. What she says. I did worse than that. I did horrible, filthy things."

"Here?" Peter asked him. "Did you do them here?"

Big John shook his head. "No, no, no. That's why I went away. I couldn't fight it anymore. I left so I would only hurt heathen children." He was pleading. "You know they don't have souls, not real ones. Of course it was wrong to . . . do things to them, to harm them, but not so wrong, right, Dad? God can forgive me? Maybe you can forgive me?"

I felt sick. Nathan still gripped my arm, and I tried to pull it free. "I'm going to puke."

"Go ahead," he said. "Puke away. Just don't leave."

I realized he didn't want me to bear witness to Big John. He needed me for himself, to share his heartsickness. He needed not to do this alone. "OK." I touched his hand. "I'll stay until it's over."

Silently, Nathan started to cry. Big John also was sobbing in loud, self-pitying, slobbery gulps. Peter stared down at him. Then he turned, reached back, and took the gun up off the table. Almost abstractedly, he wiped it clean. He pulled down his shirtsleeve, and holding the slide through his cuff, he handed it, grip first, to his shattered boy. "End it," he ordered, ignoring the muzzle pointing directly at his own chest. "Judgment is now, Ezekiel, or you damn us all along with you."

"No, no, no, no," whimpered Big John, "God will absolve me."

Peter's mouth twisted. "It's time to find out. End it. End it now."

Big John took the gun. Nathan started to pray. I wrenched myself free of his grip, leaned forward, and covered his ears with my hands. I could at least do this. "Close your eyes," I told him. "Oh fuck. Close your eyes." He pressed them shut.

Peter reached down. I could not look away. His hand still covered by the shirt, he turned the gun around. Gently he supported his son's hand. "Finish it, Ezekiel." He was whispering now. His voice like a prayer, an absolution. "Atone, my son. Wherever you go, I will see you again. We will be together for eternity in the sunshine of our Lord."

Big John looked up. His face cleared. "Forgive me, Daddy," he said, suddenly quite calm. Then, obediently, he pulled the trigger.

OF COURSE, THE WOMEN cleaned the room. Even Deb, shaking with shock and grief, swiped with a Cloroxed rag at the blood spatter of her dead son. I watched for a while, and then went upstairs. Whatever might have been between us that morning was finished. I stood under the shower for a long time. It didn't help.

The men had carried Big John's body out to his truck. I'd watched from the window as they drove the gray Freightliner, missing the driver's steps now and the front bumper, back up the driveway and away. Peter was determined to leave it off property, as if that would help anything. In a couple of hours, fast as a speeding warrant, the farm would be swarming with

Feds. I'd given Nathan a number to call, and the phone to call it with. It was a hotline, but I was sure they'd get routed through. Homeland would have their agent, and most of the fertilizer still in the back. That part of the story would be over.

I took some clean clothes from Hannah's pile. She was right—they were too big. I washed and wrung out the black headscarf. It would never seem clean. I would have left it, but there was a chance I might use it again. I rolled a blanket and stuffed it in my bag. I wanted to leave that place more than I'd wanted to leave anywhere. I no longer feared them. They wouldn't pursue me. They'd be glad I was gone. And I was angry; how dare they force me to witness their drama? To act in it? I felt as if I'd pulled that trigger myself. As immersed as I'd briefly been in their lives, I knew my own doom would overtake me alone and far away.

I walked down to the Quonset. The laptop was still plugged in by the wall. I took it. I looked around but saw nothing else I needed. Then I went over to the shed and chose a pickup. I took the one Nathan had driven to Dairy Queen. I set my bag on the floor, turned the key, pulled out, and headed up the driveway.

Hannah was standing outside the house, watching me steal the truck. I stopped and waited for her to come over. Through the window I said, "People are going to ask you about me. You'll want to turn me in. Nathan won't forgive you if you do that. Protect me and he'll be grateful." She looked thoughtful. "You won't see me again," I promised. "He's yours, if you can make it happen."

She nodded. "OK," she decided. "I'll tell the others. And I'll wash the sheets. Wipe down what you've touched." She looked as if she'd rather burn it. "We never saw you." She turned away. "Go with God," I heard her say, the "straight to hell" clearly implied. And so I left the farm.

45

MIKE

BODY COUNT

The call came through the main switchboard just after 1500 hours. LuAnn's phone rang. She listened and said, "OK. Transfer him, please." Then, because she wasn't Gary, she put her phone on speaker and set it down on the table. Gestured for us to gather around.

"Hello? My name is Peter Arnold. I'm calling about my son Ezekiel. I believe you're looking for him."

LuAnn raised her hand, warning stillness. "Hello, Mr. Arnold. This is LuAnn Sikes speaking. I'm a deputy director here at Homeland Security. And yes. We are looking for your son."

Peter Arnold's voice again, nasal and grim. "He came home yesterday to our family farm here in Jerome. He told us . . . a terrible story. He's just shot himself." He cleared his throat. "I assume you'll need to verify that. His body is in the back of his truck on the south side of the Perrine Bridge. By the Evel Knievel monument."

I could see LuAnn calculating hard. "Sir, I am sorry. That is not the news I'd hoped to receive."

"It was God's will," said Mr. Arnold's voice. "His sins were great."

"Yes, sir. I do need to ask you about his cargo."

"The ammonium nitrate? It's there with him. We chained the trailer as a precaution, but we have verified it's not a danger."

"Sir?"

"I'm a farmer, ma'am. It's an agricultural chemical. This load has been modified somehow, for safety. It's not volatile. I expect you're aware of that." She didn't respond. He continued. "I gave my number to your switchboard. You may of course call me if you have questions. But I ask that we be left to pray and grieve in peace. My family is devastated."

"Of course. I'll be in touch, sir. And we are so sorry to learn of your loss."

Gideon caught her eye. He made some sort of gesture.

"I do have one more question. Your son was traveling with a young woman. Is she still with you?"

There was a pause. "I don't know anything about that. Ezekiel returned to us alone." He hung up.

Earl elbowed Gideon and held out his hand. Gideon ignored him. LuAnn looked at her phone. "Damn," she said. "This moves things up. We leave for Jerome in an hour." She looked at me. "Mike, search warrants. That should be a new experience for you. For the Arnold properties. Seems Mr. Arnold isn't going to invite us in. We need to look around, especially since they moved the body."

"They left him in a public parking lot," said Earl. He was consulting Google Maps. "How fucktastic. That bridge looks like the only attraction for a hundred miles."

"Yeah, well," said LuAnn, "it won't be my first forensic flash mob." She stretched her hands, the left and then the right. "This guy wants us to fuck off, but we'll do our jobs."

"He thinks we basically killed his son," said Gideon.

"If he does, he's wrong," said LuAnn. "We kept that man out of jail and gave him a way to save some lives, maybe balance out his crimes. We didn't make him a vicious pervert, and we sure as shit didn't kill him for it."

"What about Ruth?" I asked. "Do we believe he never saw her?"

"Who knows," said LuAnn. "We'll see what we find in Jerome." She gathered her things. "Should we locate Ruth, the priority is to stop her feet."

"Detain her for debriefing?" I clarified.

"If she were willing to talk to us, she'd have made contact already. I said stop her feet. Bring her in. Bagged, boxed, whatever it takes."

I didn't say more. But I thought I might be warming the wrong bench. I noticed Gideon watching me. Slowly, he shook his head. Earl leaned over, tapped my arm, held up his screen. He had googled "how to apply for a legal warrant." "I'm here to help," he said, and snickered.

"Cute," said LuAnn, "but we have our own court. It's a slam dunk, but you still have to do the paperwork."

46

RUTH
OVER THE BRIDGE

To leave Jerome is a simple choice of cardinal direction: north or south, west-ish or east-ish. The bad guys were coming, and I had to assume they were coming for me. Time to bust a move. But I had to make a mistake first. So instead of choosing my route, I drove to the alfalfa pivot where Nathan and I had sat together to eat our Blizzards, one long day ago. I occupied myself finding Big John's pornography stash on the laptop. I made myself look at each kid's face and did not delete the photos. I archived them and named the file "ishouldbegladhesdead."

I waited almost three hours in that field. More than long enough, I thought. They'd have parked the truck, made the call, returned to the farm. Surely they didn't stop to run errands. Peter hadn't even washed his hands after directing Big

John's suicide. If Nathan were going to look, he'd have found me by now. There was nowhere else I could be. We wouldn't finish that conversation. I got out of the truck, walked across the field, and tied my headscarf to the control box on the central tower of the pivot. Then I waited a few more minutes. I don't know what I wanted. Maybe for Nathan to ask me again to stay, even though I knew I could not. He didn't come.

What I did not want to do was turn south and retrace backward the road Big John and I had traveled. But that's what I did. If Homeland was searching for me now, they would not expect it. If they weren't, crossing underneath them was the best way to avoid an accidental run-in. I assumed Peter had left the truck somewhere away from the farm in Jerome. So I got back on 93 and turned toward Wells. As I approached the Snake River, I saw what I had missed asleep the other way at night—the Perrine Bridge, a massive four-lane truss bridge that carried the highway over the canyon a quarter mile to Twin Falls. Traffic was backed up almost half a mile. I pulled into line and crept forward. What did I care, after all? I had nowhere to be, no one waiting. Absorbed in my self-pity, I didn't notice the two young men until they tapped on the hood.

"Yeah?" They were wearing blaze-orange jumpsuits and backpacks. They carried helmets. Not cops, probably not Christian farmers or terrorists. BASE jumpers.

They looked at each other, back at me. The shorter one said, "I'm sorry. We were just wondering—would you mind if we jumped in the back to ride across? They closed the walkways, and our car is back at the visitor center."

"What's going on?"

"No idea," he said. "Someone thought they found a body. Perrine is down to one lane in the middle and no pedestrians. No jumping either, unfortunately." He smiled his best smile. "We won't delay you much—we just need to be dropped in the parking lot."

"OK," I said. "No problem. Hop in the bed."

"Thanks!" they said in unison. I rolled up my window and drove slowly out onto the bridge.

A problem with almost-flat country is that you can't see a cop until you're right on top of him. South central Idaho is shitty getaway country. As it was, I was trailing larger trucks, and my view forward was obscured. I saw the roadblock when we were less than ten cars back. Two men were taking a cursory look into each vehicle and waving it through, alternating directions. One was some kind of municipal cop with a holstered pistol and a safety vest. The other was Hydrant Mike.

All I could think, as I drove helplessly forward, was he must have shat where he ate in some irretrievable way to be the guy on the bridge in the late-day heat, checking cars. His fancy-footweared feet had to hurt. Well, I thought, his luck was about to change. I wasn't even wearing shades. I took a grip on the wheel and stared straight ahead. *It's over, over, over* rang in my head.

We were there. The traffic cop said something to the BASE jumpers. I heard them joking, "What's a couple more bodies, officer?"

A long moment. Then a tap on the window. I rolled it down, still staring ahead. *Over, over, over . . .*

"Miss?" I turned my head and met his eyes. I saw that he knew me. He looked older and like he hadn't shaved for weeks. "Sorry for the inconvenience," Mike said. A curl of paper dropped into my lap. He stepped back and motioned me past the roadblock. I glanced at my lap. The note had a phone number and two words, scrawled in a hurry: *Ruth RUN.*

47

MIKE

PROOF OF LIFE

did it. I saved her.

48

RUTH
ENTER BLOBS

f I didn't vomit when Peter preached Big John into shooting himself, it made no sense to do it then, when Hydrant Mike let me go. I risked a glance in the rearview mirror. He'd turned away to look into the next car. I tucked the paper in my pocket. Thinking would have to wait. Right now, my job was to drive without hitting something.

Across the bridge, the entrance to the visitor center parking lot was blocked by police cars. I saw Big John's truck parked in the northeast corner. It was swarming with police and crime-scene technicians. There were bomb-squad vehicles and an ambulance with its lights off, something on a gurney in a black body bag. Big John's masters had reclaimed him. Some movement behind me, bright orange, caught my eye. I'd forgotten my hitchhikers. I pulled to the shoulder and waved the guys out. "Sorry," I said. "I can't take you further." I tried to act naturally but also not to turn my head. They jumped out thanking me and headed off to charm their way to their car. I pulled back onto 93.

I did not go on to Wells. I couldn't make myself do it. I turned east instead and followed the Snake River. I drove slowly. My mind hurt. Everything hurt. My anonymous face felt reflected on every surface, huge as the projected head of Oz, but neither great nor powerful.

At Burley, I followed a sign to the boat docks. There was a clean restroom and a flat park where I sat on a bench and stared at the flat river. Would Big John be alive now, I wondered, if he hadn't taken my $300 and let me into his truck? I didn't know; his government puppeteers seemed pretty trigger-happy. It was a sure thing he wouldn't have been forced to suicide by his own father; that ending was securely in my column. Except the vile predator part. I supposed he'd earned that bullet on his own. Still, Peter could not remember me fondly, or Deb. It would have been impossible, I thought, to join that family. Even ignoring my bad temperament, God and agriculture aside, Thanksgiving would have been unsurvivable. I wondered what was happening now. How long before a hundred boots crushed the young barley, hunting my traces in the dust.

It was nearly sunset. A woman walked with her dog down to the edge of the water. She ignored me and stripped her clothes into a pile. She wore a red swimsuit underneath. She pulled on a rubber cap, settled her goggles, and waded into the water. Her dog ran back and forth, then stood poised by her clothes, paw raised, waiting in silence as she swam out and eventually back, her strokes rhythmic and confident. She nodded at me as she walked back to her car, her dog celebrating around her feet. I could not just sit like a lump, counting off my mistakes. I had to do something.

I booted the laptop. First I needed to alter the record of its cellular adapter so it could not be traced. It took a while to find that database inside Homeland Security. I cloned the record for Big John's old phone—I knew that wouldn't activate. Now I was back online. My laptop wasn't anonymous, but it wouldn't show up on any internal government search. I was a girl in a park with a computer. Somewhere a vast automated transfer paid the bill. As I configured my encrypted call anonymizer, I wondered again why I'd involved Thom in the initial plan. I thought about our trip to Cayman, all that shaved ice. I'd paid a lot for marginal assistance. But even discounting for nitwittedness, Thom had paid more. Things seemed to be ending badly for all my adventure buddies. Big John was gone. But maybe Toby and Thom were still somewhere I could reach. Maybe I could still help the Arnolds. There was a chance I could redirect my pursuers.

I hate all that visualization shit, but I tried to use it now. I put myself elsewhere—anywhere but Idaho. I called Gideon and he answered immediately.

"Ruth!"

"Hey!" I said, as cheerfully as I could manage. I imagined a window seat in a teahouse. The walls were egg-yolk yellow. Unremarkable local photography on the wall, with aspirational price tags. "I'm just checking in."

"What the hell! We're tearing that farm to pieces looking for you."

I waited a beat. "Farm?"

"Come on, Ruth. In Jerome. Isn't that where you are?"

"What's Jerome? No. I don't know where that is."

I heard the click of his keyboard. He was trying to trace the call. "Ruth, you can trust me. Where are you?"

"I took your advice, Gideon. And you saved my ass again, thank you. What's this about? You told me to get out of that truck and I did. I'm safe." I stirred my imaginary mocha. No, too sweet. My imaginary latte.

"You didn't go to Idaho?"

I laughed. "Uh, no. That Ezekiel guy was sketchier than you know. The bomb was the friendly part."

"I've heard."

"So obviously I bailed. How stupid do you think I am? Isn't that what you told me to do?"

"But the tracker, Ruth. Someone hacked that server. That had to be you."

"OK, yeah. That was me. I had to negotiate my exit." I decided I needed some sort of pastry. No, a dessert. I picked a streusel crumb off my lemon blueberry cobbler. Delicious. "Seriously, Gideon, I'm not in Idaho and I never have been. If that's where you are, it explains why you haven't found me. I left Big John in Elko."

"You got off in Elko?"

"You're being nosy, but yes. I got off Big John's truck in Elko." And got right back on, but he didn't need to know that. I waved at the imaginary waiter. Pointed to my water glass. I mouthed "lemon."

Gideon sighed. His tracking was hopefully not going well. "Ruth, I need to go deal with some things. Can we talk again in a couple of hours?"

"OK," I said. "But I called for a reason. I had no idea you were picking through Germ, Idaho, looking for me."

"Jerome."

"Jerome, sorry." I needed not to push it. "I want to make a deal. I'm safe now, but I know that's temporary." I remembered to flatter him. "I won't win if you're playing."

"A deal?" His tone changed. "You want to come in?"

"'Want' is not the word. But I think you and I can work out a way to end this."

"I'm glad to hear it." I sensed him flipping beads through the six-dimensional abacus that was his brain. I was sure he'd land at yes. Who knew what he'd traded for that fake finger iPad hack years ago. He'd never turn down the power to walk through walls, virtually speaking. "What are you thinking?"

"I'm thinking I need something from you first, some sort of proof. You've had my back so far, but I need to know you can follow through."

"Ruth," he said. "Spit it out."

"OK," I said. "First I want to be sure your people didn't slaughter my friends. I want a video of Thom and Toby. I want them reading that poem "Jabberwocky" together, shirts off so I can identify them. Post it on Instagram by midnight. Then we can talk about a next step."

"Nice, Ruth. But midnight? That's a little tight."

"We're negotiating, Gideon. This is the part where you counter. I don't need to call you if the game is me talking to myself. I can do that here over coffee."

"Midnight tomorrow. Remember, I need to find them first."

I was pretty sure he'd done that already. He didn't seem like a loose-end kind of guy. It wasn't his look. But I didn't think he could plausibly fake all those weird words with both voices and the video in just over a day. In a way, I already had my proof of life. "Midnight tomorrow. But the slower you move, the more chance I get zipped into a black bag before I spill my secrets."

His voice was dry. "You are the hide-and-seek champion of the world, Ruth. I'd never bet against you. Have you got a hashtag for me?"

"Sure. Just use #ThomAndToby. I'll see it. Thom with an *h*; no *e* in Toby."

"I can spell their names, Ruth."

"I know you can. I'm not so sure about your helpers."

A long silence. "Maybe my helpers could meet your helpers sometime." I heard him close his laptop. "We'd be unstoppable."

"Maybe," I said. "We can talk about it after you post that video."

"Have a good night, Ruth." He sighed. "I need to go save some religious farmers now. I'm glad you're safe. Really, I am."

"Good night, Gideon. And thank you." I summoned the waiter, whispered, "Check please." I'd done what I could tonight for Nathan and his family. And for #ThomAndToby.

My next call should have been to Hydrant Mike. Instead I searched "animal shelters near me" on Google Maps. I found one less than a mile away. It was late, but I dialed anyway. Twenty minutes later, a tired young woman with a kind face was unlocking the door for me. "I was still here feeding," she said. "I'm Melissa. You're welcome to come in and meet everyone."

"Sorry to be so late. I'm driving cross-country," I said, "and I realized I can't go further without a dog."

She laughed. "It happens like that. Maybe someone older?"

"Yes," I said. "Perfect. I need an experienced copilot."

I should say I wanted them all, but nothing caught me until the last kennel. It was an aged mutt that eyed me in a resigned way, barely swinging his tail so he could say he tried. He was certain I couldn't want him, and that conviction won my heart. Melissa guessed, "Something squatty crossed with something sleepy? And a whole lot of blob."

"Hairy blob," I said. "I promise to take care of him. Please, please trust me to take him."

She sighed. "I believe you. And honestly? He's been here a year. People don't want the old weirdos."

I wrote fake information on her paperwork. She gave me a bag of food and some medical records. And Blobs, on a cheap leash, looking incredulous.

"Are you stopping in town for the night?"

"Oh." I looked at Blobs. "I guess I need a dog-friendly place now." I'd planned to drive until I could not, then sleep in the truck. Not dog-friendly.

"I have an Airbnb," she offered. "Available? Down the road? If you want?"

Blobs and I waited while she finished up. We followed her to the rental. "I'm just next door, if you need anything," Melissa told me. "There's a box pizza in the freezer." She smiled at me, hugged the dog, and was gone.

I locked the door, put my bag on the table, set a bowl of water on the floor, and sat down. Blobs lay by the wall and watched me with a subdued wariness.

"You're my prisoner now," I told him. "I hope you decide that's a good thing. But you weren't exactly swamped with alternatives." I pulled out the laptop and started it up. "I need to make a call. I have to stay alive now so I can feed you." I couldn't run forever, I realized—I had the wrong dog for it.

I'd been trying to imagine what bureaucratic plotline had put Hydrant Mike unshaven on that bridge, and what state of mind had made him let me go. Obviously things sucked at work. Catching me could have changed that, but he'd looked past me. More than that, he'd warned me off. Try as I might, I couldn't see the trap. I dialed the number from his note. Waited while the software routed me twice around the moon.

"Hello?"

I had no problem getting government cheese to take my calls. "Mike."

He released his breath with a huff. "Finally. Are you safe?"

"Yes," I said. "I owe you for that. Thank you." I still couldn't place him in this setting. He still seemed like the same annoying sales guy from years ago. It was like going for a root canal and seeing your fourth-grade bus driver holding the drill.

He sounded testy. "I was surprised to see you on the bridge. I did not expect that."

I noticed he didn't use my name.

"Idaho was a poor choice."

"I had my reasons," I said.

"Did they hurt you?"

"No. Those farmers are good people, however it looks. If they're in trouble, they don't deserve it." Blobs had settled his head onto his paws. Getting comfy while he waited for bad news.

"Most people don't deserve the trouble they're in," snipped Mike. I'd annoyed him, defending the Arnolds. I wanted him not annoyed for this conversation.

"That's true," I said. "You're right."

I heard him shift the phone against his ear. His voice warmed slightly. "What's your next step?"

"My plan depends on you, Mike. I called to say thanks, but also because I want to make a deal."

"A deal? With me?"

I said, "I think I can give you what you want, without your people needing to dissolve me in a barrel."

"Maybe," he said. "I hope there's a way. But we have to be careful. I'm on your side. But don't trust anyone else, no matter what they promise you."

I wondered if he meant Gideon. "Will they even let you do the right thing? It seems like they don't appreciate you much."

"That's mostly for show," said Mike. "It's more complicated than you think."

"OK," I said. "I believe you. But I need a favor first."

"Just tell me how to help." He sounded sincere, this man who had stomped into my life and kicked everything to shit. Hydrant Mike was definitely the hero in his own drama.

"I need to buy gas safely. I need to get groceries. That stupid news story is forcing me to hang with a bad crowd. I'm learning new words." Blobs was asleep; I lowered my voice. "Ugly things happen when you make me barter with bomb builders and sex criminals, Mike. It doesn't enhance my patriotism."

"That was not my idea. I tried to stop it."

"Well, it's time to try harder. What do you think happened when that psycho truck driver saw my face in the paper? It was luck he let me off just messing with the tracker. You built this bus, and then you threw me under it. Do you expect me to die to protect a bunch of government networks?" I'd pushed my voice louder. Blobs startled awake. He flattened his ears. Mike was silent. I went on, quieter. No scaring the dog. "It's been a long time since you and I met. I want to trust you. But I need some kind of token. If I'm going to work with you to end this, you have to get me a retraction first. That's my ask. That's what I need to move forward."

"A retraction?"

"Look it up in the dictionary. You know what I mean. Accused killer exonerated. Whatever it takes. Pay them again, the people you paid before. Give me my face back. It'll be safer for everyone." Blobs scrabbled to his feet. He stretched awkwardly, one leg at a time. He looked at me, then at the door. "When my innocence is front-page news, I'll know you're ready to deal. I have your number." I hung up before he could reply.

I took the dog out. He snuffled cautiously around the yard. I wondered how long it had been since he'd walked on grass. He moved under a bush to do his business. I looked into the night sky. I knew two constellations so I found them—Orion and one of the dippers. Big John had died. The force that had set him over me had failed to deliver. He was dead and I was alive. More than that, I was through that roadblock, and less alone than I'd been that morning; I had acquired the old dog to share my future biscuits. I stood in the dark for a long time, waiting for him. Eventually he came over and stood looking at me. He'd accepted that I ran the door. We went in together, and Blobs took a sloppy drink and lay down. I baked the pizza and tossed him chunks of crust. Then I locked the door and pulled the shades and went to bed.

49

MIKE

OPEN SEASON

My instructions in Idaho had been to stay out of the way. The arrangement had suited me and LuAnn. She didn't want me mixing in. And her shortsighted aversion had allowed me to stand in the one place I thought Ruth might materialize, though the odds had seemed so slight that I was still in a state of suspended self-congratulation that my hours breathing exhaust on hot asphalt, granted in comfortable shoes, had yielded such a spectacular result. Ruth had come to heel, at last. Life outside my protection had taught her the value of my sheltering presence. Someday, we might both find humor, and a silver lining, in our miserable days of separation.

I called an Uber to drive me out to the Arnold farm. It was

late, but I knew the team would be on-site, jacked on adrenaline and overtime, wrecking the place acre by acre under floodlights. When I arrived, I found the search wrapping up early. Our team was loading equipment, taking down lights, U-turning their SUVs across the planted crops in preparation for departure. I walked down a long driveway and found LuAnn standing with Earl, Gideon, and two sour-faced men in hats. She was giving them papers to sign, approving the destruction. The older man was signing, and the younger one was telling him to read everything first.

I went up to Earl. "What's happening?"

"Sherlock Holmes has manifested another miracle photo. Apparently your girl never made it to Idaho." He looked at Gideon, who shrugged like his brilliance amazed him, too, and handed me a printout. It showed a young brown-haired woman, head down, crossing under the camera. He had marked it up with colored arrows like a *Line of Duty* prop.

"Based on biometric calculations, there's a 96.7 percent probability the woman in this photo is Ruth," said Gideon. "The time stamp is twenty-two minutes after the truck left Elko. She was never in Idaho." He was daring me to challenge him. And I could have. His reference measurements—her height, her weight, even her shoe size—had to be guesses, if not outright fabrications. As a factual matter, also, I knew he was wrong. What was he doing? I looked up and caught the younger of the two men in hats, presumably an Arnold, giving me a hard look.

The man dropped his gaze and said, "You don't need calculations. We've told you Ezekiel arrived alone. We aren't criminals."

Everyone ignored him. LuAnn said, "You know her best, Mike. What do you think? Is it her?"

I pride myself on a grasp of the big picture. I'm not generally distracted by minutiae or the need to appear right. So I considered my answer. I knew it was not Ruth in that photo. She had been here, and continuing the search might prove that. Several white pickups sat parked across the yard. Probably one was missing, and proper police work would yield a plate number that could lead them to her. Which I did not want. I would be bringing her in myself. So I studied the photo. "It certainly could be Ruth," I said. "I can't prove it's not." I looked at the younger Arnold, who was now staring fixedly at his boots. "I see no reason these folks would lie about her. They called us, after all."

"Way to take a stand," said Earl. "It *could* be any twenty-something brunette."

"The math is more precise than that," snapped Gideon. "It's not a matter of opinion. We need to go back to Elko and track her from there."

I looked at Gideon and thought it was a good thing Ruth had called me and not him. Her instincts might be improving.

"Ma'am?" I turned to LuAnn. "If you have a minute, I'd like to update you on a separate topic."

She sighed. "Can it wait? No?" She handed the paperwork to Earl. "Wrap this up, please. I'll see you back at the hotel." She turned to the Arnolds, offered a handshake between them that both refused to notice. "Let me say again, we are sorry for your loss." She turned to me. "Come on, then."

We walked up the drive together and got into one of the SUVs. I refused to talk in a government vehicle. There would be no more rookie mistakes. At the hotel, we sat outside by the butt can. I told her, "Ruth called me about an hour and a half ago. She wants to make a deal."

"How thrilling—the phantom speaks. You'd better tell me."

I repeated the substance of the call, including Ruth's complaint about the news story.

LuAnn said, "I did tell Gary that story would backfire. He thought we needed an excuse to terminate her on recovery." I expected her to move, but she did not. Her hands stayed folded, like they waited for orders. "We don't really need an excuse to shoot her over at Homeland. Things go wrong all the time in the field."

"It would be better if she could train us to use her backdoor. Access would be strategically valuable."

"Yeah, yeah," LuAnn said. "It's hard to see why she'd disclose anything, at this point."

"I'm sure the proper incentives . . ."

"We are not bribing a thief. It sounds like she doesn't need money, anyhow. And we couldn't risk releasing her, once we caught her."

A bribe was worse than a bullet—good to know.

"I'm sure you're right," I commented respectfully. "'An ever uncertain and inconstant thing is woman.'" I heard my misstep at once and added, "That's Virgil. And I meant Ruth, not you."

"I'll say one thing, Mike—you don't suck up much, do you?"

I decided to take that as a compliment. I asked, "What do you think about printing a retraction in the meantime?"

"Oh, I'm fine trying that. Why not? It sounds like an excellent project for your man Gary." She took out her phone. "I'll text him now. Certainly cheaper than a huge manhunt, if you can bring her in with a news story."

"I expect she'll contact me again when the story breaks."

"I hope so," said LuAnn. She sent her text and put her phone away. "What do you make of Gideon's new photo from Elko?"

I worded my response carefully. "I think it's right to continue the search. But I don't believe that photo is the key to locating Ruth."

"So it's not her."

"Ma'am, I don't know. I think it's important that Gideon believe we trust him, regardless of that photo's authenticity, or his motive in discovering it just now."

"You know," she remarked, "Earl says Gideon is too far ahead of us too much of the time."

"Well," I said, "there's a chance Gideon is really good at what he does." I didn't want common cause with Earl, even if it improved my standing.

"That's possible. But if you're right about him, he has a personal interest in finding Ruth on his own."

"Yes, but he'd need her alive and talking, not minced in a body bag."

"True." She sat a moment. "You know my family had an outfitting business? I paid for college with guiding tips. I made sure rich, drunk men tagged out with trophy bulls." I wondered if I had a new habit of fidgeting or if it was only that LuAnn herself sat so still. She went on. "Sometimes they were so impaired, I'd have to sight the elk myself and pull their finger on the trigger." She turned to meet my stare. "A tanked hunter may forget the date or who pissed his pants. He'll remember if he didn't make the kill shot, and then he won't tip."

"Is that even legal?"

She rolled her eyes. "Not the point."

"You don't care about fair chase?"

That made her laugh. "Fair is different up the mountain. Everything there had a job. My job was to shoot an elk for the client. The elk's job was not to get shot. Usually I won, so now I'm here." She stood up. "You know I don't enjoy the thought of killing that girl, Mike. I just have a job now too, and I'm a realist."

A realist trained on game trails, I thought. Hard not to treat every creature walking toward you as a target.

50

BLOBS IS MY COPILOT

One of Thom's hobbies had been lucid dreaming. He felt he was missing out on crucial stories and ideas while he slept, like there was a hole in his brain pipe that needed plugging. I'm a student of the opposite discipline—I would forget half my waking thoughts if I could, and dreams are much worse. I can mostly control my own mind in daylight. Overnight, the doors slam open. I won't describe and will try to forget what I dreamed that night in Burley, Idaho. I woke early, scared to my bones and sick at heart. I didn't remember where I was. I only knew there was no point being there. My breathing changed, or I must have moved. Anyhow, I made enough noise to rouse the other sleeper. I heard a scrambling sound, and sixteen toenails clicking on the laminate. I rolled over to see Blobs, who'd slept against the farthest wall, on his feet, studying me.

"Hey," I said. He took a few steps toward me. He might have wagged the tip of his tail. Hard to judge on a fat, hairy dog what is wobble and what is micro-wag. I took it. "The good news is it's today, not yesterday," I told him, and took him out. I was tempted to stay the day in Burley, hang out at the docks with my dog and spend another night. I rejected that plan as careless. I'd taken a chance on Melissa not being a newspaper reader. Last thing I needed was her waking up with the sense she'd seen me somewhere before, then meeting me again and realizing where it was. Not to mention those few days in Jerome had left a mark. I packed my things, stripped the bed, and washed the dog bowl. I didn't steal anything. On the table, I left $2,000 with a note: *This is not drug money. Thank you for the dog.*

Blobs kept to himself by the passenger window, but he seemed to like looking out. He relented enough to eat half my meal when I stopped for a burger at Carl's Jr. After that, he sprawled across the bench and fell asleep. "I will win your heart with junk food," I told him. I drove east through more arid cropland with pivots crouched over low dark frilly plants that I guessed to be potatoes. Nathan would have known. I gave myself five minutes to wallow in shapeless regret for his absence. Then I reminded myself there'd been no choice that would have put him here, playing name that crop from the dog's seat. At best, I'd be baking biscuits in a dusty tiny house, watermeloning my way through a headscarfed offline life.

At Farmington, I pulled into a rest area, and we sat over-looking the shriveled Farmington Bay of the Great Salt Lake. I took out my laptop and started the day's to-do list. Item one: Hydrant Mike payback. It'd taken until last night to decide what to do about him. I hadn't remembered him at all until his creepy cameo in the Ops Center, but I was starting to blame Mike for a lot of my shitty situation. So I'd decided to sacrifice what remained of the Caymans account. Twenty-five million was a sickening payout; it felt like a celebrity divorce, minus the celebrity and the divorce. But I'd refined my dream of wealth to include moving freely behind my own face. I reminded my-self that life was about more than money; what money could buy also mattered.

My job got easier when I found my chip in the Caymans bank firewall. I broke into their account server, which was eas-ier than logging in and figuring out how to erase my tracks. I located the account I'd shared with Thom and set about modi-fying it. I deleted any record of my name or Thom's as joint account holders. Hydrant Mike, formally Mike Whitterfield Jr., retroactively took possession of the prize. Now I had a story to explain why he'd let me operate so many years without inter-vention: I'd been paying him off. Then I realized my pursuers were unlikely to find my other accounts in Belize and Switzer-land; this Caymans account could stand for the whole haul. Mike could have been the puppet master from the start. In fact, he could have forced me to do the whole heist. I'd make him regret those bugs.

I left Thom's transaction records but modified the transferee. I carefully screenshot the account and the transaction history. People would believe Mike had withdrawn all that cash, I decided. He had the right mix of vanity and obliviousness. I could be the next tiny bitch pissing on his shoes. The hole in the story would be Thom's mattress stash. I'd erased its provenance, assigning the withdrawals to Hydrant Mike. I thought for a while but couldn't resolve the problem. I decided it didn't matter. Offshore bank records were hard to obtain. It was going to be awkward to expose Mike as it was. Possibly they would overlook the lack of forensics when they got to poor Thom. Probably he'd confessed to save them the research. And it would be fine if they had to let him off, as long as the uncertainty didn't trickle over to Mike's crimes. I didn't wish Thom further harm.

I checked my work carefully, got off the server, saved copies of my screenshots, and shut down the laptop. Blobs was watching me. "That's one," I told him. I'd planned to force my dog to walk thoughtfully along the Great Salt Lake, but the bay felt toxic and depressing. We got back in the truck and drove on toward Salt Lake City.

I stopped for gas in the smallest, crappiest station I could find. Living on cash meant paying for gas inside, sometimes over a rack of newspapers. I'd noticed the smaller stations had fewer papers, and would set them in a corner to use the counter display for candy and tobacco products. Their cameras, if they were real, were usually out of order. It would require a wild series of chances for someone to pick up my trail from a gas stop. Still, as time dragged on, I became more afraid of people. Now that I had Blobs and a plan for escape, my fear of recognition and arrest became almost unbearable. Fortunately, the Salt Lake metropolitan area was riddled with Walmarts, each with a self-checkout and the budget store etiquette of not looking closely at fellow shoppers. The woman in a raincoat and slippers buying two five-gallon buckets of rainbow sherbet did not scan my face for any criminal likeness. She had problems of her own.

So I bought some protein bars, a foam bedroll, and a cheap sleeping bag; a dog bed, dog bowls, dog food, and dog treats; a giant rain tarp. I remembered project Please Blobs Love Me and added a rotisserie chicken. Then I went online, booked a spot at Wasatch Mountain State Park, and took Blobs truck camping. I was lucky to find there was cell coverage, since I hadn't remembered to check. I found my site, parked, and made Blobs go for an amble. I was determined he should take walks, and he was more determined he would not. He controlled his legs, so he was winning. We compromised on slow snuffling circuits with me admiring the view, pretending to be patient, and him ignoring me completely until I gave up and offered a treat. Then we went back to the truck. He snoozed and I returned to my work. I thought Gideon might have been able to locate me, with enough information, the right guesses, and a lot of time on his hands. But Gideon was under deadline with his video assignment. Even he couldn't do everything at once. And Mike was negotiating with newspapers, so he wasn't at liberty to invoke whatever Angel of Dumb Luck had thrown him into my path on the Perrine Bridge. Most straight men are deeply and unconsciously transactional. They believe that patience and a few odd tasks will deliver title to any woman. My pursuers were focused on the chores that would allow them to claim the storyline damsel; they weren't watching for her to come mucking about behind their firewall.

Item two on my to-do list was research for exposing Gideon. Leave-no-footprints stuff. I wasn't ready to modify anything. I expected him to detect my changes when I made them, so I'd need to be fast and accurate. First, I prowled through the Homeland tracking server to see what had changed and where the logs went. I'd left myself a private login, which was handy since they'd patched the bug I'd used when I'd hacked in for Big John. I made notes and looked out the windshield at the view. Blobs turned around and lay back down with his head in my lap. It was peaceful, more what I'd imagined for my wealthy life: office with a view, sleeping dog, snacks. Check, check, check.

I located the acquisitions database and tried to figure out how my chip had become ubiquitous in the government networks when Hydrant Mike and Gideon had both been onto me, probably from the design phase. I could see from the reporting history that Hydrant Mike had been asking the same question. I prowled through backups and email logs. I saw that Mike had initiated a prohibition on my chip well before it cleared beta test. He'd been so sure it was compromised, without the slightest notion how. Not that he was wrong; still, his incomprehension seemed embarrassing. Someone had removed that line item right after he'd created it. Someone skilled at self-concealment, with a healthy aversion to getting caught. I made detailed notes of where I should have found those records. Then I backed quietly out of the Homeland network and closed the laptop.

"Chicken time," I told Blobs. He gladly roused to eat. We watched the sunset, and I rolled out our bedding in the back of the truck.

At midnight, I went online, logged onto Instagram, and checked #ThomAndToby. Gideon's video was up. It wasn't slick. I suspected he'd managed the whole thing himself and filmed it on his phone. I watched a couple of times. I'd chosen the poem mostly because the nonsense seemed hard to fake, but also because I'd wondered how to pronounce several of the words: hard *g* or soft in "gyre" or "gimble"? This interpretation didn't settle that question. Thom looked puffy; I guessed he hadn't achieved the deal he'd imagined. Toby seemed to be getting some sunshine, slightly more the beamish boy than his partner. Something about their body language made me think they weren't sharing many poems these days. Love and thieving is a tough mix; love and getting caught was probably impossible. I downloaded the video. If Mike failed, I might need it. Then I updated Blobs. "I'm pleased to inform you I'm no longer a double murderer." He seemed indifferent. I should have called Gideon, but I put that off. It was late. Let him wonder. I heaved my dog into the back of the pickup—he was heavier than he looked. Then I climbed in after him and went to sleep.

51

MIKE

A MASTERSTROKE OF BUSYWORK

I returned to San Francisco and summoned Earl. It was time to show Ruth some leadership. We found an IT guy and took him to Gary's computer. I'd decided to handle the retraction myself. I'd spent my travel time picking through surveillance stills, looking for the right image to accompany the article. There could be no doubt this time, I was speaking to Ruth directly. This portrait might someday take pride of place on our mantel, whenever she was free again to join me.

Earl was jittery, even more than usual. "You cleared this with Gary?"

I lied. "He's on vacation, I think." I knew he never came in before nine, especially with an urgent assignment pending. "LuAnn briefed you on the plan to retract the murder story?"

"It was a stupid move from the get-go," said Earl. "Forcing your girl to serve bad actors was perverse. That driver was a sleaze." I liked him better sucking up. He'd probably aced that class in consulting school.

"Here's the email thread," said the tech. I looked over his shoulder. I needed all the newspaper contacts and some idea what we'd paid the first time.

"Send that to the printer," I instructed him. And then I added, "Reset the password so we don't have to call you seven more times. Murphy's Law and all." I scribbled the new password on a sticky note—my birthday. No one guesses obvious passwords anymore. Gary would have to call for help.

Earl drummed his fingers on the desk. If I still knew him at Christmas, I thought I might get him a pair of tap shoes, or maybe morris dancing bells. Alternatively, a straitjacket and a set of hobbles would also be appropriate. "Come on," I told him, "I want this story in print tomorrow."

I made him carry the printouts. As we walked together down the hallway, I glanced out the window and saw Gary, crossing the parking lot with his briefcase.

"Not on vacation after all," Earl said.

"Huh, odd. I was sure I saw his name on the calendar." I pressed the button for the elevator. "I guess we know how he'll spend the morning." I liked the thought of Gary failing to log onto his own desktop. He should know how it felt to be locked out. Earl pushed the Close Door button twice and got us to the first floor.

We made a call list, and Earl contributed background percussion while I worked the phone. Negotiating the retraction of Ruth's double-murder headline was so difficult, I thought it might be easier to get her a new identity and put her through witness protection. Placing the fake story had been the easy part. Gary had exhausted the available reserve of editorial corruption, and it seemed virtually impossible now to set the record straight. Eventually I threatened to place another article, a true one, about three-letter agencies planting fake headlines. That threat got progress—that threat and the rest of Gary's discretionary budget for the year. By tomorrow, Ruth would be publicly exonerated. She would be further in my debt and on her way home.

52

NOT OUTDOORSY
IN THE LEAST

Blobs and I learned together that camping would not be a shared passion. It was early. It was also chilly, and the damp air hung with a whining curtain of starved mosquitoes. I hustled us both into the cab. Then I crept out to rescue our gear. Blobs hunched sadly on the seat, pawing at his muzzle. He furrowed his old eyebrows, looking every day of his unknown age. "I'll fix it, buddy," I promised him.

So instead of calling Gideon—I imagined him sprawled sleepless on a chair in his lab, phone in hand—I scrolled through the Salt Lake City For Sale by Owner ads for camper vans. I could have found something within my cash budget that at least expanded our enclosed space, but my rich self, enraged by the forced march and steady diet of processed junk, drew the line at a cat-pissed rust bucket. I found an aged listing for a nearly new gray Winnebago Travato that looked clean and well maintained. Then I located a wrecking yard that would take a vehicle without a title. At eight o'clock, I called the number from the classified, and we headed out to take a look.

The owners were a younger couple. Their driveway was cluttered with expensive toys: two Harleys, a Honda side-by-side, a Sea-Doo on a trailer. They watched me anxiously as I went through the interior. The van was overpriced and they knew it. It was also perfect. Gray was my color.

"I like it," I told them. "I also know you're five thousand over market." They exchanged one of those couple-ish looks that meant one of them agreed with me. I said, "I'm not going to ding you on price. What I want to do is to wire you payment in full. That's going to take a couple of hours. In the meantime, I need you guys to follow me to the salvage yard so I can sell this truck. When the transfer clears, we can do paperwork on the van, and I'll drive it out of here." I looked at the rear bumper. "And if you could, remove the stickers. I'm not a marathoner." I hoped the international wire would follow my personal law of wealthy banking: the larger the sum, the faster it would move.

The woman asked, "Are you getting divorced? Is that why you're junking your pickup?"

"Something like that."

"We aren't Mormon," she told me.

"Well," said her husband, "we kind of are. What she means is we don't judge."

They both looked judgmentally at the pickup. Leaning on the half-open window, Blobs gazed judgmentally back.

"We'll sell it to you," the woman said, as if there had been a chance they'd refuse. "I mean, look at your dog. He wants it."

And you need the money, I thought. I said, "He for sure does, and it's all about the dog. Can I use your Wi-Fi?"

It was a large transfer, but there was no way for an observer to prove it was mine. I didn't think the maybe-Mormons had recognized me. If they had, they wanted to sell their van more than they wanted to turn me in. It was oddly easy to spend almost $100,000. Type, click, done. Two weeks earlier, I'd been too cheap for the fair-trade coffee.

A better person would have found a way to return the pickup. I hadn't meant to steal from Nathan. I thought about calling him. Then, just for a moment, I imagined their story if I hadn't come into it: Big John would have kept his commitment to Homeland Security and the explosives bust. Maybe he'd have been released from service and returned to the farm. More likely, his cohorts on one side or the other would have winged him "by accident" and sent him home in a box, a hero. His people would have had their boy either way, and their pickup, and no experience of the nighttime search-and-destroy mission that must have followed Ezekiel's suicide and my escape. Peter would not have turned that gun around; Nathan would never have fallen down the fantasy manhole of being with me (and I wouldn't be grieving my twenty-four hours of almost being wanted). I'd been a blight on Jerome, Idaho, and that was saying something.

So I didn't call Nathan. I did keep his license plates and

later, at a rest area, swapped them onto my new camper. Ghost tags would be a later project. Blobs entirely approved the upgrade. He had no reservations about acting rich. He rode panting in the passenger seat until, exhausted from staring out the windshield, he moved back to sleep on the bed.

I got to Laramie in the late afternoon. Time to stop procrastinating. I took the Snowy Range exit and bought gas at a Big D that advertised BURRITOS AND AMMO. Then I drove north under the highway and pulled onto the shoulder. I took out the laptop and called Gideon.

"Ruth? For fuck's sake, I thought you were dead."

"I have a tattoo: if found dead, please call Gideon at this number."

"What if I get a new phone number?"

"It's a QR code."

He laughed. "You sound well, anyhow."

I heard kids' voices in the background. "Are you at work?"

"I'm always at work." I heard him shift the phone. The noises dropped away.

"Sounded like you were performing community service."

"No," he said. "I've been performing your service instead. Did you see the video?"

"I did."

"Toby took some persuading. He's no longer in custody and wasn't eager to play."

"I bet," I said. "Cookie for Gideon, getting it done."

"Screw you," he said mildly. "You wanted to try. I'm just telling you I tried."

"I know," I said. "Thank you. I'm glad they're alive. You told me, but I wanted to see for myself."

"I'm sure you did," he said. There might have been an edge to his voice. "So . . . I need to warn you, we've hit a snag in our agreement to bring you in."

I had not agreed to come in. I didn't correct him. "What's that?"

"The deputy director at Homeland. She's taken over the operation. She thinks you have no reason to work with us. She may call in the snipers."

"She's never had to live on Wawa burritos," I said carelessly. I heard him register the localizing information and try to decide whether it had been an actual slip. "Or Love's," I added.

"Or Pilot sushi? No, probably not." He sighed. "I'm going to figure this out, OK? But I need some time. I need to convince her we can trust you."

"Ask me for something."

"What?"

"Let me convince her. Tell her to ask me for something."

"What sort of thing? She can't demand a million dollars. The optics are bad."

"I'm serious, Gideon. Ask her what she wants. Better yet, arrange a call and let me ask her."

Long silence. Then he said, "Let me talk to her and see where we get. Call me tomorrow? Five p.m. Be prompt."

"Let me check my schedule."

"Ruth."

"Fine," I said. "Five tomorrow. I'll call you." I hung up.

I looked at Blobs, who was chewing a non-rawhide treat on the bed. I wondered why my particular goon team thought it best practice to threaten my life every time they asked me for something. "If I were a man," I told my dog, "the ratio of stick to carrot would be reversed."

Probably Gideon thought it was me versus him; he needed to win, so I had to lose. Maybe he'd reassess when he learned I could fight back. I was sure he had a lot to hide, though I was finding his secrets hard to uncover. I'd found no trace of his interference in the acquisitions that had spread my chip through the federal network infrastructure. But who else knew about the backdoor, wanted it deployed, and might have planned to exploit it? Gideon had probably expected me to offer him the access sequence. I knew it had to be his intent to compromise the US networks, but he'd left no trace. It had been serious work for me to manufacture the records that retroactively proved his bad behavior. Gideon was a skilled adversary. I hoped when he stopped underestimating me, he might see the advantages of an alliance. In the meantime, I needed to write an exploit for the chips I knew about, in case his boss played rough. I drove a few minutes further north and found a little pull-off. The van let us stay anywhere. The whole country was my parking space.

53

MIKE

AENEAS HAD FAITHFUL ACHATES— I GOT STUPID EARL

Earl was a version of Gary with a massive operational upgrade and no institutional loyalty; he was the Reddi-wip to Gary's half-and-half. Except Earl was not my boss, and I liked Reddi-wip. Every classical hero had at least one faithful, capable cohort to support him in his mighty deeds. Without complaining, I'll note that my own colleagues never met that standard. Earl managed to be entirely in my business without doing any useful work. He was particularly interested in what would happen after the papers published my story.

"So you expect Ruth to make contact?"

"Yes."

"She's just going to call you at work? Like, honey, don't forget the oat milk, and by the way I'm turning myself in?"

"Something like that, yes."

"Why?"

I gritted my teeth. "Why what?"

Earl gave me what he imagined to be a disarming grin. "I just mean, why would she call you now? You're removing the pressure. She's managed to evade us so far. What would bring her in?"

He was fidgeting around my desk as I coordinated with the different newspapers. Bit of a slow learner with women, I decided. "She's alone for the first time," I told him. "She doesn't like it. She's used to my protection, even though she didn't know it was there."

"'Baby, it's cold outside'? That's what you think?"

"More or less. That's a crude way to put it."

"What makes you think you protected her?" He held up his hand. "No, no—don't get mad. I'm not being critical. I'm just trying to join the mind reader's club. It seems to me that she might associate you more with the pursuit than the safe time before it."

"Ruth is smarter than that. Sure, she ran initially. She hadn't seen me in years, and the setup spooked her. We went in with weapons, remember? But she called me when we were in Idaho. She reached out, and she didn't have to do that. We were nowhere near finding her." I had not and would not tell him about the encounter on Perrine Bridge.

"Hmm." He'd taken an actual quarter out of his front pocket

and was walking it back and forth on his knuckles. Tweedle-dum was in fine form. "So let's say she calls you. What's the plan? She comes into the Agency to teach a continuing-ed class on walking through firewalls?"

"Obviously it's more complex than that. But yes."

"And then? Pleads guilty to her big bank heist and retreats quietly to the federal pen?"

I shifted in my seat. "We're not completely naive." But the answer, of course, was yes. It had become obvious that Ruth would need an attitude adjustment, a time-out, as it were, to ensure future reasonable behavior.

"We?" He put the quarter away. "So LuAnn is on board?"

"Of course she is."

"Easy, cowboy. It's just you've got a history of, let's call it autonomous improvisation." He patted me on the shoulder. "Glad you're managing up this time around. What's LuAnn's angle?" His tone had changed. There was even a note of respect, perhaps.

"LuAnn shares my view that there's a bigger trophy loose in the woods."

"Such as?"

I hesitated. He could make a strong ally, but he had a history of stealing my credit, and I needed this win. He guessed my thoughts. "I won't horn in, Mike, I promise. I won't stand between you and the sun. But I want to help. I'm paid to help you succeed, right?" He looked sincere. Then he snorted. "Actually, I get paid no matter what."

The man was an ass, no doubt. But LuAnn seemed to listen to him. I took a breath, and then I told him the story: my discovery of Ruth's compromised chips in our network, the mysterious deletion of my entry on the acquisition blacklist, my suspicions of Gideon, and my plan to use Ruth to prove his traitorous activities.

Earl furrowed his brow. "I can't say I follow all that, but I agree that Gideon is up to no good. And if you're wrong about Ruth, well, it's not my career, is it?"

That was as close to an oath of loyalty as I could expect from a man like that. I took it.

54

RUTH

LITTLE PIES ON THE PRAIRIE

The bed in the camper van was much better than the bed of the pickup; I still slept poorly. It took effort to forget what passed through my mind when I did. Finally, I gave up on resting and lay quietly into the early morning. Blobs had crept up off the floor and was snoring with his head by my foot.

I heard a car drive past outside, then another. I got up and peered out the windshield. A trickle of traffic, more cars than I'd expect anyhow, came along the back road and turned east at the intersection ahead. There was a banner I hadn't noticed yesterday, stuck out in the cow pasture. It was red with white letters and read BAKERY. I roused Blobs. "Come on, buddy," I told him. "Life has new purpose."

I talked him into a short walk along the median. Then we drove down to the bakery. It was in a red steel outbuilding next to a small red steel house stranded out in a large dry pasture. There was a sign that said GOLDEN PRAIRIE BAKERY, a few chairs around small tables, and a line. The case was stacked with fresh baked goods; the air smelled of coffee and scratch-made pastries. I smiled at the lady in front of me. She smiled back and I asked her, "What's good here?"

"Everything," she told me. "They don't make it if they can't kill it." Words to live by.

A young man handled orders and the register. Behind him, I could see an older woman with a hairnet rolling out piecrust on a floured marble slab. She reminded me of Deb. I bought three fruit hand pies, a sourdough boule, and, thinking of my dog, four pizza rolls. I remembered I was rich and added a coffee. As the boy counted my change, the woman who was not Deb looked up, saw me, then gestured to someone around the corner. An older man walked around to look at me. He nodded to her and they stood for a moment, shoulder to shoulder, staring. So I learned that Mike had delivered on the newspaper story. I also realized I'd been overconfident in my anonymity.

Blobs and I ate outside at a small picnic table. I drank my coffee and picked at a hand pie; he horked down two pizza rolls, then lay quietly by my feet, considering his fortunes. Today I would split between driving and writing more scripts. I was turning back, driving west. We'd spend the night again somewhere near Salt Lake. I needed to call Mike, but it felt wrong to call from a place I'd already been recognized. I was squirrelly, and it was still early in San Francisco. I drove west on I-80, finally stopping in Rawlins. I checked a paper and there I was, in my own hair this time, absolved of guilt. It was a new creepy photo, this one taken inside my apartment. I looked like I'd just woken up. It's not possible for me to look porny, but that photo was damn close. I wondered at Mike doubling down on the stalker vibe right when he needed to make me play nice. Then I saw his stupid dragnet, right in the first paragraph: a fabricated police spokesman attributing my exoneration to pressure from a fictional online group all using the hashtag #RuthRun. The story claimed the hashtag would now be repurposed to celebrate justice. I looked on Instagram, and a photo was up already. The man behind me at the bakery had snapped my picture, tagged and posted it. The van was out of frame, fortunately, and Blobs partially so. It was impressive how he managed to look like he was not my dog, even sharing snacks. But anyone looking would know where I'd been ninety-three minutes ago. It would be a competition to find and photograph me. People knew I was safe to approach. The tactic was smarter than I'd expected from Mike, more of a Gideon move. My stomach turned. They must have communicated long ago about my visit to the lab. I hadn't considered a stronger allegiance. I started the van and impulsively turned north onto 287, away from the interstate. It was an hour later, rolling past the ghost town of Jeffrey City, when I realized I was only somewhat afraid. Mostly I was angry.

I had no cell service until Lander. There I parked by the public library and generated a pool of new Instagram accounts. I named them Never_Ruth1 to 100. Then I wrote another script to collect photos of women and post them through the accounts, all tagged #RuthRun. Anyone named Ruth, any average-looking girl. For the next hour, I googled photos of women and patched my shitty scripts. They wanted tips? They could have them. Let Gideon sort through the metadata for proper dates and likely locations. Social media wasn't my skill. Social anything wasn't my skill. But I might slow him down. I couldn't remove that first picture, and I knew he wouldn't miss it. There were only so many ways out of Laramie. All I could do was try to bury any further sightings and stay hidden.

Taking 287 had been a stupid impulse. From Lander I could only turn around and backtrack south to I-80, or continue north through Jackson, the looky-loo capital of Wyoming, onto winding, exhausting roads south and eventually west to San Francisco, first traveling Highway 93 for miles through Idaho, straight past Jerome, and again over the Perrine Bridge. Probably that would trigger an exorcism. How small was this stupid country that all roads led to Jerome? I took three deep breaths. I was tired. I was also overdue to call Mike and behind on my list. The day had gone sideways, I decided, because I'd relaxed my food discipline. I blamed the hand pies for my misery, the hand pies and Gideon.

It was almost noon. I turned around. At four thirty I stopped at a Bureau of Land Management property near Park City, Utah. I'd decided to bundle my calls to Mike and to Gideon. I thought it might help me detect their collusion. I called Mike first.

"Ruth!" It was the first time he'd used my name on a phone call. It was a clue. To something.

"Hello." There was too much ambient noise. He had me on speaker. "Thanks for the article. I feel a lot safer." Because why not.

"Oh," he preened. "I'm glad." He coughed awkwardly. "So," he said, "I know we talked about you sharing the access sequence to your chip." I waited. "Of course that is still a *top* priority. But the timing may be complicated."

Blobs was loudly slurping a paw. "Yeah?"

"Of course it is *essential* that access to your chip be limited only to a very few people . . . the right people. It's a real need-to-know information asset."

"Yes?"

"It has come to my, to *our* attention that we have a highly placed individual who should not be privy to that information."

"Mike," I said, "pick up the phone. I can't see who else is in the room." I heard him take me off speaker. "I need a name."

"Leave it to me," he said.

"A name, Mike. I need to know who I can trust. And maybe I can help."

"OK," he said. "It's someone you met, a long time ago? In the lab? A hairy guy. Do you remember Gideon?" So it wasn't Gideon in the room with him, or Mike was practicing his superspy double cross.

"I remember him," I said. "Do you want to renegotiate?"

"Renegotiate how?"

I spelled it out. "I remember Gideon as being careful, and

skilled. He won't be easy to catch. A guy like that doesn't leave evidence, but I could fix that."

"Ruth?" said Mike. "I'm muting the phone for a second. Hold on." He managed it. And unmuted me without hanging up. "Yes. We'll take you up on that offer. What do you need?"

"Time," I said. "Give me three days. I'll get you enough to make a case against Gideon. And Mike?" I could tell he'd put me back on speaker. "Tell your boss to stand down the snipers. I have a script running against my deployed chips. If I don't manually reset it, things get prehistoric."

"No need for threats," he said stiffly. "I think I've proved how far you can trust me." Which was funny, in a way. Then he said, "I saw you fake your tuition payments and never turned you in. I kept your secrets before they were valuable, Ruth."

I couldn't stop the question. "You what?"

"That's how you caught my eye. I watched for years before you saw me. Wind beneath your wings, you know. If you're honest, you sensed I was there."

Which I had not. I'd have thrown myself off the edge of this flat earth to escape him, had I sensed his presence. My ears rang. I felt a strange charge right to the tips of my fingers. I'd planned to ruin him already. It wasn't enough. Now, I'd tear him to pieces and burn them one by one. He'd regret surviving it.

"Ruth?"

I realized I was still on the call. I said, "Three days." And hung up.

I looked at Blobs. Seven years that man had stalked me.

That villainous panting bastard. How had I not known? What would I have been, had I never stumbled into the sticky web of Mike's obsessive need? A thief, yes, with a microchip obsession—that was all me. But my flash of enlightenment in Gideon's lab, Mike's grimy prints were smeared across it now. The stink of his following breath tainted all that came afterward. I wanted to peel off my skin. And Mike's. I reached for Blobs, and he backed away—not an emotional support animal. "I won't allow this," I told him. "I'm going to obliterate him."

It was a few minutes before five. I had to call Gideon.

"Ruth," he answered right away. "You're everywhere today." So he was following #RuthRun.

"Call me Waldo."

He chuckled. "The first one was pretty good. But even you wouldn't have collected a dog."

I said nothing.

"I suspect someone is regretting that social media strategy right now."

I made a mental note to check Instagram. I asked, "Did you get with LuAnn?"

"Yes," he said. "She's here."

"Can I talk to her? What do I call her?"

"Ma'am works. Do you need me to spell it for you?" I waited. "I'm putting you on speaker now," Gideon added. "Please don't do anything crazy." Which hurt a little, even though I knew he was performing.

I said, "Ma'am, please don't say anything significant. This call isn't secure. I'd advise you to go buy a new, sealed burner phone. Unpack it and hold the label with the number up in front of the parking camera behind the Agency building. I'll be watching, and I'll call you on that phone."

She had a generic Mountain West drawl, with a layer of DC authority. "Are these theatrics necessary?"

"Yes, ma'am, I'm sorry but they are. I'll explain when we can speak in confidence. Anyone that's with you now stays with you, and please don't share the new phone number."

"Fine," she said. "I'll expect your call."

Gideon came back on the line. "Ruth, what the fuck. You know this call is secure."

"I don't know that," I said, "but it doesn't matter. I need to promote myself. I'm working on my marketing."

"Your marketing is a huge pain in the ass," he said. "Which is on brand, I guess. Do you mind sharing your plan?"

"It's what we said," I told him. "I'm coming in. I just want to know I'll be safe."

"I want you safe too," he told me. "You know that. I have to go. I'm escorting the deputy director on a critical mission to 7-Eleven."

"Look both ways before you cross," I told him. I hung up and logged onto the Homeland Security server to bring up the parking lot livestream. I'd noticed it when I was researching acquisitions. So far, so good. Gideon wouldn't have the opportunity to find his way onto our call.

She was back in twenty minutes. She was playing it straight. Whatever listening scheme Gideon must have proposed, LuAnn was confident she could handle me on her own. Or she already suspected what I would tell her. She was tall, strong, and very blond. There would be no arm wrestling. I zoomed in on the image, grabbed the number, and called her.

"Ma'am. I apologize for the extra miles."

She said, "I understand your concern, I think. You're satisfied we aren't being monitored?"

"I am," I said. "Thanks for taking my call."

"You've wasted a lot of time already," she said. "How about you tell me what you want, and what you can do for me."

I took a breath. "I can give you the people who hacked your server to hide Big John's tracker, and who spread my compromised chip into your infrastructure."

"People?"

"Yes. I've identified them. I'd need some more time to get you appropriate documentation. I was never trying to hurt my own country. I want to help fix that."

She stood, considering. She was completely comfortable on her feet. I watched her on the livestream—she hadn't walked away. She was thinking through what she knew or had guessed, trying to decide if my offer matched her instinct. I wondered what would have happened if she had crossed my path instead of Mike or Gideon. I had a hunch I wouldn't be hiding in a camper van on an anonymized call, breathing dog farts. She said, "How much time?"

"Three days."

"And you want?"

"To walk away. Just let me disappear."

She laughed. She looked up at the camera. "People don't actually disappear, Ruth. Not people like you."

"I don't want to go to jail," I told her. "And I don't deserve to be shot. I'm not a traitor."

"I need to think about this," LuAnn told me. "And you need to deliver. I'll promise you a fair chance, anyhow. I won't lead you into a trap."

"I can live with that," I said.

"Do you want to give me names?"

"Follow your gut, ma'am. You don't seem like a blame-without-proof person."

"You're right about that," she answered. "Or a trust-without-proof person. I'll keep this phone on and charged. If something happens, call me. Otherwise, I'll expect to hear from you in three days. Same time."

"Yes, ma'am. Goodbye." And I watched as she hung up, tucked the phone in her pocket, and walked away.

I set to work falsifying the evidence to convince LuAnn. I forgot to feed myself; I forgot to feed Blobs. At ten p.m., he shoved his nose into my hand. I looked up and he pricked his ears. "Sorry, buddy," I told him. "I suck." I remembered Gideon's snark about the dog and thought this must be what he'd meant. I scooped out kibble and refilled his water bucket. Then I thought about Gideon's other comment and logged into Instagram. #RuthRun had more than ten thousand tags—people had picked it up, made it a game. I scrolled through the photos—lots of random women, a gnome, two gerbils, some dogs. I was waiting for Blobs to finish eating so I could take him out. There were cars, beer, lots of plain brunettes like me, a couple of dick pics, and then, all the way back at the beginning, right after the spamload of images from my fake accounts, a photo of two Dairy Queen Blizzards, side by side. It had been posted by a new user, Nathan_in_Jerome. He'd tagged it #RuthRun, of course, and #CallMe. So he did have a phone. I sat in my van, looking at the photo, listening as the dog licked the memory of dinner from his bowl. Then we went for a short walk.

Very late or very early, I couldn't say which, I crawled out of bed and went back to the laptop. I worked my way onto Mike's work computer and uploaded Big John's filth into a huge hidden directory. I password protected it with Mike's birthday. He seemed like a guy who'd think that was clever. It would take them maybe ten minutes to find that directory, once they started looking, maybe another sixty seconds to access it. "Fuck you for everything, Mike," I said, and went back to bed.

55

MIKE

DUTY BOUND

I hung up the call and thought briefly of Aeneas, torn between love and destiny, how "he [felt] care in his mighty chest, and yet his mind [could not] be moved." I would be firm in my resolve. I hoped Ruth wouldn't veer off track and do something else silly. My control still felt tenuous.

Earl was wound up. "She sounds young," he said. "Do you believe her? Can she do it?"

The question seemed simpleminded, even for Earl. Ruth had technical mojo. If she needed to get into something, program it or snoop it or whatever, she would figure that out. I was the idea guy; she handled implementation. I'd judged her when she involved Thom. I'd assumed she was going soft, never that she needed help. Now, I expected her to deliver strong proof of

Gideon's bad behavior. I would use her evidence to convince LuAnn, to secure my status in the Agency, and to soften the impending consequences for Ruth's own crimes. Dido ended poorly, but I'd always believed she could have survived Aeneas's greater calling with a little patience and supervision. Aeneas could have founded Rome just as well with his lover alongside. Ruth would have to go to jail, of course, but it could be a nicer one, and the term should not be overly punitive. I would hire her when she got out, hire her and more. I had forgiven her already.

"I need to brief LuAnn," Earl said. "I mean we. We need to brief her and make sure . . ." He looked at me.

"Make sure LuAnn doesn't have Ruth killed before she delivers Gideon?" I asked.

"Exactly," he said. "And more than that, Ruth needs to give us access to that chip. It's embedded in the network perimeter of twenty-four foreign governments."

"And ours," I pointed out.

"Well, yes," he said. "Gideon needs to be stopped. He should pay for what he did. But we can't overlook that foreign uptake was probably influenced by our own deployment. Other countries follow our lead, you know. And soon we'll control the means of access." Lacking a table, he tapped a stupid little rhythm on his watch face. "Baby, bathwater. I told you we should wait to take her, and I still think I was right."

"I suppose," I said. I would have watched her for years longer, if Earl hadn't materialized and pressured me to round her up. I wondered again why I was in the doghouse when my project was so strategic. Complex operations always had an element of disorder. When Ruth turned herself in, that would make me whole. A happy ending would overtake the messy middle. All would be well.

We didn't have a chance to brief LuAnn together. In the evening, she called us to her office to announce that she would personally handle all further communication with Ruth. Gideon was there, sitting silently to one side. When she called us in, one by one, he came out looking angry and left without speaking. Earl was next, and I was last. My interview was brief. She sat at her desk and took notes with a different Montblanc—a StarWalker Metal Fineliner in blue. I wanted to compliment her taste in writing implements. We shared an appreciation for fine pens. I did not find the opportunity.

"Please don't repeat what you've already told me," she said. "I just have a couple of questions."

"Ma'am," I said. "Anything I can tell you, I will."

"Yes, I know. Four different ways. There's no early history in Ruth's file. What's her background?"

"I don't know." I was going to explain my ignorance, but she cut in.

"Place of birth? Family history?"

"No. Her college records were falsified after the fact, and I never found her original application."

"Falsified how?"

"Father: M. Mouse," I replied. As I have explained, I hadn't wasted much effort to research her background. No history could explain Ruth, and I hadn't liked thinking about her life before I knew her.

"Ah." LuAnn tilted her head slightly. "Boyfriends? Girl-friends?"

"Absolutely not."

"Never?"

"Not recently. She's been too focused for that."

"Well," said LuAnn. "You can watch a thing for a long, long time without understanding it. That's all. Thank you. And, Mike?"

"Ma'am?"

"I doubt she'll call you again, but if she does, you send her to me. No more sneaky bullshit."

"Yes, ma'am," I said. But she was wrong, another clueless bureaucrat. I knew Ruth would call me again. She couldn't quit me.

56

RUTH

MORE MISERABLE MILES ON I-80

spent the next two days mostly working on my new software. I resented scripting and wasn't good at it. Chip design is meditative. It's world-building in miniature. You identify constraints like size, power, required functions, and standard interfaces; the rest is a solo collaboration between you and physics. A good script, on the other hand, is like a sorority social secretary. It has to account for variation in everything around it. If a tree might fall in the forest, the script must anticipate it, plan to withstand the impact, or find a new path around it. I used Thom's old work for a base. It was odd, I thought, that a guy who could design work-arounds for every possible network impairment would, in the real world, stuff cash in a mattress. All Thom's planning had gone into my project. He'd been a doofus in his actual life. That turned out better for me than for him.

I looked at Nathan's Blizzard photo more than I should have, but I didn't call him. The phone I knew about had been used to report Ezekiel's suicide. It would be monitored, and the Arnolds' story was they didn't know me. Of course I could deal with that obstacle, but I couldn't solve the larger problem of what to say once a secure call went through. Our moment, if it had been real, had passed. I'd been scared, Nathan bored; no way to recapture that magic.

The afternoon of the second day, I did my laundry, emptied the sewage tank on the van, topped up my fresh-water supply, and bought a thumb drive and a small printer. I went to Walmart and made a tag for Blobs with Melissa's name and number on it, just in case. He and I shared a pint of vanilla ice cream, looking out over the Wasatch. I should have started driving but didn't want to stop overnight in Elko or Winnemucca or Fernley. I hated I-80 now and could barely stand the thought of traveling it again. Instead, I prepped for my meeting with LuAnn, everything but modifying the logs on Homeland's networks. Gideon would be watching them, I thought. A man so meticulous about brushing away his tracks had to be monitoring everything all the time. I rehearsed my story and hoped LuAnn would let me walk away. I'd considered trying to take her out, but it wouldn't have been right. Mike and Gideon deserved it; she did not. And I was a little bit afraid of LuAnn. I took a shower in my tiny van bathroom and tried to nap. Well before midnight, I packed up and headed west toward San Francisco.

It was a brutal overnight slog. I wished again for the chance to remake my choices, to have vanished gracefully before Mike came stomping in to ruin everything. I was feeling richer with my dog and my fancy van, but we still dangled over a doom pit. Life was not yet classy.

Just past eight in the morning, I stopped at the Boomtown Casino and called LuAnn from the parking lot. The asphalt was already hot. In a nearby RV, a couple was fighting, and a baby wept without energy, on and on, like it didn't expect a response. A very blond woman threw up carefully next to her pale pink Cadillac. It was a beautiful day.

LuAnn picked up. "What is it?" Cuddly.

"I'm on track," I told her. "I don't want to meet at your office. There's a park southeast of there. It has a baseball diamond and a playground."

Her voice was very dry. "I'm aware." She took a moment, then continued, "My son will be at Little League in that park today at five o'clock. As I'm sure you know." Damn it. I hadn't meant to threaten her.

"I'm sorry," I said. "I actually didn't know. I found it on Google Maps." I paused. "I was looking for a place to walk my dog."

"OK," she said. "We'll go with that. Better bring a dog, then. Make sure you clean up after it. We wouldn't want you apprehended for a poop violation. We can meet by the bleachers."

"Yes, ma'am. I'll see you at five." She hung up. I considered calling Gideon, who would be watching the calendar and the phone. But it was probably better to have him thinking I'd bolted than to have him looking for me in San Francisco. I called Mike instead.

"Ruth?" So his third party was in the room. They were getting an early start.

"Yes. I'm calling to set a meet."

"We'll be here at the office. Just call up from the desk when you arrive."

I was tempted to ask if he'd validate my parking slip. I said instead, "That's not how I want to do this. You and I have some things to discuss privately. I'll meet you at Draves Park, at five fifteen this afternoon. Do you know where that is? Meet me at the playground. We can walk to the office afterwards."

He hesitated, but I knew that dumb fuck wouldn't pass on a chance to see me alone. "Yes," he said. "I know where that is. I'll be there."

"Come alone," I said.

"Yes, alone," he replied. I hung up.

57

SAILING INTO CARTHAGE

I got off the call determined to get rid of Earl. I was not having him chaperone my rendezvous with Ruth.

"She's playing you, dumbass. You're fucking up beyond belief." Here at last was an authentic opinion, even though it was wrong.

I put my cell in my pocket. "Are you finished?" I needed to shave and to retrieve Ruth's violin. I'd thought about bringing flowers, but the violin would mean more. It would recall our shared history, if she got jumpy. It was time to clip the figurative chain onto her fine leg. I didn't expect her to like it right away. I planned to quote her Aeneas's speech to his men despairing on the island, right before Venus intervenes. "Hold out," I would tell her, "and save yourself for kinder days."

Earl said, "Stop and think, Mike. Please. If she intended to turn herself in, she would meet you here."

I'd had about enough of Earl. I told him, "I'd fire you if I could. I'll settle for telling you to fuck off instead." He looked startled. "Get out, Earl. Go tap the table in some other office." He didn't move, so I stomped away. It was less impressive but better than staying another moment to hear his ignorant advice. I had to wait around the corner until he left before I could go back for my dopp kit.

58

RUTH
VENGEANCE

I drove my van to the park and circled for half an hour, looking for a space. By the time I parked, I felt pressed for time. If it had been my own scripting to prove out, I'd have been in full panic. But my work had been mostly a modification of Thom's, so I set up the laptop, crossed my fingers, and executed the scripts. I watched for errors, then opened a second window and called Gideon.

"You're cutting it close," he said. "LuAnn values promptness."

"I stopped to see my dealer, and it took longer than I planned."

He sighed. "You're a hard person to help."

"When did you really try?" I was off plan. All I'd meant to do was to occupy him at his desk.

"What's that supposed to mean?"

"It means Mike told me he's been stalking me since I was in college. Which makes me wonder what you knew when I walked through your door that day."

Gideon's voice turned cautious. "Ruth, I didn't force your hand in any way. No one did."

"Give a lot of tours in that lab, did you? Weekly demonstrations, open to the public?" I checked my other window. Still no errors. Slowly, I was reconstructing the evidence he must have removed, one by one placing his fingerprints back where he'd wiped them away. I added log entries to establish, reestablish, his role deploying my chip to compromise US networks.

"You know we didn't," he said. "But Mike told me when you showed up I should demonstrate our work."

"You didn't ask why?"

"Of course I did. He said you'd know what to do with it. He said, 'Paint the door and watch her find it.' Those were his words."

"What the fuck did that mean?"

"I don't know. It made sense at the time. Now it just sounds stupid. But this is ancient history. I need to know that you're coming in today."

"I am," I said. "I'll have them call up from the desk. I'll be there about five thirty, assuming LuAnn hasn't shot me first and hung my head on her wall."

"She knows I want the access sequence first."

"Well then, I'll see you soon," I said.

"My lucky day," said Gideon. "I'll wear something pretty."

I should have rung off. Instead I said, "Have you ever considered going freelance?"

"What's that mean? No. Why?"

"Just that maybe we could team up. You said it, you know, we'd be unstoppable."

And then Gideon laughed. It wasn't a jolly, loving-life, ho-ho kind of laugh. It was a nasty I-know-things-you-can't bark, and it went on. "Ruth," he said at last, "I would rather run a shovel at the local landfill than work with you. You're not that smart. You're a shitty thief and a terrible liar. Everyone who helps you gets fucked. You're going to jail, and I'm going back to my life. That's how this ends. All I'm willing to do is try to stop you from getting yourself killed."

I was surprised, and also not—why would Gideon be different? I should have kept my friendly thoughts to myself. "I think you're supposed to wait to insult me. I think your genius self still needs something I have." My voice only shook a little. Blobs was lying by my seat, and I nudged him with my foot. It was just us now. I promised him a steak when this was over, one of those fancy ones drenched with brown butter, tender for his old teeth, with fries on the side; Blobs loved curly fries.

"I'm sorry." I heard keys tapping. Probably he was googling "how to apologize." "Look, Ruth, I shouldn't have said any of that. It's not even how I feel. You know I think you're amazing. I'm just worn out trying to keep you safe. Please tell me you're still coming in."

I lied. "I'm coming in." Then I hung up on him. My scripts

were finishing. I thanked Thom again for his good work, poor bastard. And I congratulated Gideon on his psychic powers: he had helped me, now he'd get fucked. We'd find out who was smart and who was not.

I printed out the fresh log records and Mike's fake bank statements, burned everything onto the thumb drive, and stacked it all in my fruity Walmart shopping tote. I really needed to buy a nicer bag. It was a quarter to five. I leashed Blobs. I'd considered letting him stay behind, but if my meeting ended badly, he might be stranded indefinitely. I imagined him waiting in the van until the batteries died and the AC quit, staring at the door, thinking I'd abandoned him. "Sorry, buddy," I told him. "You're my plus-one for doomsday." We walked together very slowly across the park. It was a dud as far as city parks go—all sports and no food. There wasn't even a hot dog cart.

We were on time, but LuAnn was early. I assumed at least half the spectators milling around were steel-jawed undercover agents ready to intercept and neutralize me or my savage companion. I wondered about her definition of the word "trap." She stood next to the bleachers watching the field. I walked up behind her. "Ma'am?"

She turned. "Ruth." She saw Blobs. "Oh. You really did bring a dog."

Blobs wagged once, uncertainly. He was well past his steps quota for the day just coming from the van.

"And I really do have a son." She pointed to a boy, probably eight years old, in an oversized shirt and cap, facing the wrong way in left field. He seemed to be counting clouds. On first impression, he lacked his mother's remarkable focus.

I said, "It takes a while for some kids, doesn't it? He'll come around."

LuAnn looked at me, surprised. "I don't give a shit about baseball," she clarified. "He just wanted the cap." She looked again at the boy. "He's doing math in his head. Or thinking about supper."

She turned back. "Shall we?" We walked together away from the bleachers, my dog hanging on the leash, the fake parents drifting casually behind. LuAnn stopped. "Well?"

I handed her the two stacks of paper and the thumb drive. I said, "I think these records will corroborate what I'm going to tell you. There are two men who have been working together."

She pocketed the thumb drive and tucked the papers under her arm. "Talk me through it."

I braced myself. Blobs lay down in the grass. I said, "In my defense, and I think you may know this, I met Mike when I was nineteen. I thought I was too smart to get trapped by someone like him." I checked her expression. "And I was poor. I don't know if you've been poor, but when Mike offered me a way to make real money, I didn't second-guess it. I knew he worked for the government. I thought it was OK." Her eyes narrowed. I needed to be very convincing. "I'm not a stupid person, but I did a stupid thing, and by the time I knew what was happening"—I made a helpless gesture—"I couldn't see a way out of it."

"So, the chip was Mike's idea, and he had you design it." She was watching my face.

"In a general way. He said he needed to walk through fire-walls. He doesn't understand the specifics, obviously. I didn't know he planned to rob banks. He told me I was serving my country. I know this sounds idiotic in hindsight. When I fig-ured it out, I challenged him. He told me he could put me away forever. He has an account in the Caymans where he had me send the money. It's all in there." I indicated the papers. "I was afraid of him for a long time. But eventually I couldn't take it anymore. So ten days ago, I told him I was done. I took down the bank transfers, he came after me, and I ran." I couldn't read her face. I went on. "It was bad luck I ended up on Big John's truck. I was just trying to get out of Sacramento. But when Big John told me to disable the tracker, that's when I realized my chips were in the Homeland network too. And then your server went down, right when I needed help." I looked at my feet. "Chips are my thing. I'm not great with software. Anyhow, when the tracker deactivated, I realized Mike had to be work-ing with someone a whole lot smarter than he is, and it seemed that person was also trying to get to me, probably wanting the access sequence for that chip." I met her gaze. "That was Gideon, ma'am. He's been talking to me right along. At first I thought he was helping me get away from Mike, but they're in it to-gether."

"And what do you think they have in mind?" LuAnn asked. A muscle worked in her jaw. I had her. Honestly, I'd nearly con-vinced myself. I realized that if this version of events had been true, I could have stopped running. I might have stayed, learned from this woman, quit hiding. For an instant I wanted that so much my teeth hurt. Then I remembered my remaining $200 million and unwanted it.

"I don't know," I told her. "But they've punched your network full of holes. Whatever they want and whenever they want it, they can take it. I wish I had more for you, but I don't."

"You've done what you promised," said LuAnn. "The cleanup is my job. And you're overestimating the threat on our own networks." She sounded amused. "Unless, of course, there's some reason your super-chip can't just go in the dumpster. Money and a trash can solve a lot of problems." She studied Blobs, then me. There was a moment, a look. I wondered if in fact she'd bought my story. Maybe it just suited her agenda.

She stood with her back to the baseball diamond. It was something in her posture, the way she concentrated on me. I said, without thinking, "That's not your son, is it?"

"Of course not. And this is not your dog." LuAnn stooped to Blobs, turned his new tag up between her thumb and forefinger. "I'm sure Melissa was glad to help out." She straightened up. "Careless." I didn't answer. She said, "I think if you were a super-spy you'd be somewhere else, doing something else. So I won't make you my hunting trophy or try to send you to prison. I doubt there's much left to prove against you at this point." She looked thoughtfully at my paperwork. "If I offered you a job, would you take it?"

I shook my head. She seemed to expect that. "Fair enough. But I can't let you just walk away." She put her hand in her pocket. It was just the phone. "Consider this the Bat Signal. If it rings, you answer it. Understood?" I took it from her. She said, "I don't suppose you know where those two men might be at the moment?"

"Mike thinks he's meeting me right now over at that playground," I told her. "And Gideon will be waiting for me at his desk at five thirty."

LuAnn offered her hand. I shook it. "I halfway wish your path had turned a different way," she said.

"I do too, ma'am." I almost meant it.

LuAnn gestured at her dead-eyed agents. She said something into her watch, pointed toward the playground. I watched them move off to intercept Mike. I thought I could see him, waiting like a dumbass over by the slide. He might have been holding my father's violin. Surprise, fucker. I hoped he was scared.

The phone had been a nice touch. Some Bat Signal. It was intended to distract me from the fifteen minutes I'd given them alone with the camper van, my laptop, and everything else I owned. I stood for a moment, stunned by my mistake: leaving my van by the park had been stupid. Worse than stupid, it was unrecoverable. We couldn't drive off now.

"Come on, guy," I told Blobs. "We need to go." I lobbed the phone into a trash can and turned to walk the other way, out of the park. Blobs dragged hard against the leash. I was thinking ahead, planning our escape. We would take a bus, and another, then find our way to some used car dealership. We could stay in the car until I found another RV. I pulled on the leash. Blobs sat down.

Dogs have a narrow range of expressions; his face said "fuck you."

I could hear commotion behind me. They were rounding up Hydrant Mike. How long could I stand here, alone and unmoving, before LuAnn changed her mind, noticed me stranded in the open, and could not resist the shot.

"Get up!" I jerked again on the leash, and Blobs lay down. I pulled hard and shifted him a few inches. He whimpered then, not loud, just a hopeless old-dog sound. I wished he were reasonable, or portable. I couldn't carry him, and dragging an old dog across a San Francisco park would get me mobbed. I stared down at him. He gazed past me. Waiting for snacks, maybe, or wishing he'd never met me, most likely. I didn't even have an Oreo to offer him.

I tried setting him on his feet. He had no usable lift points—anything that looks like a handle on a dog is not designed for carrying. He lifted his head very slightly. He looked at me, finally, and he growled. It wasn't a big growl; we both knew he wasn't about to go Cujo. We also both knew he meant it. "I have to go," I told him. "Come with me, Blobs. Please. Please come with me." I let go and he dropped his muzzle onto his paws. He sighed.

And so I left him. I looped his leash around a bench leg and walked away. I walked off across the park, looking for a bus stop. I was hungry, but eating had to wait. At least I was still rich.

ACKNOWLEDGMENTS

I wrote this story on a challenge from Lynn Festa, years after re-nouncing all publication fantasies. The process that took Ruth from an overreaction to a novel (with a Penguin tramp stamp!) has re-quired an extraordinary alignment of incredible people.

My first thanks go to Lynn, for unbreakable friendship and provoking this exercise. Next, to my good friend Ian Shapiro, who read several versions and believed my silly story ought to become a book. Ian passed a draft to the great and generous writer Jonny Steinberg, who actually waded through a stranger's manuscript and pitched it to Nicole Aragi. That introduction was a staggering piece of luck for me. Thank you, Nicole, for your insight, your kindness, your advocacy, and your humor. Thanks to Kelsey Day for logistics support and vital dog enrichment. Thank you to Pen-guin Press, especially to John Burnham Schwartz, who provided

ACKNOWLEDGMENTS

crucial editorial insight and was a good sport about my rookie ignorance. Helen Rouner has been a tactful guide through the publication process.

Thank you, Buddy, for babysitting a hawk, Mary Jo for hundreds of miles, Sara for road trips (and for convincing me not to delete the entire thing), and Dr. Dana Saunders for battling the Were-Rabbit.